SOME UNKNOWN GULF OF NIGHT

SOME UNKNOWN GULF OF NIGHT

By

W. H. Pugmire

Arcane Wisdom
2011

Some Unknown Gulf of Night © 2011 W. H. Pugmire
Artwork & Illustration © 2011 Matthew Jaffee
This edition © 2011 Arcane Wisdom

P. O. Box 130
Welches, OR 97067

arcanewisdom@me.com

Book Design & Typesetting by Larry L. Roberts
Copyediting by Leigh Haig

Also published in a 100 Signed and Numbered Hardcover edition

All rights reserved. No part of this book may be used
or reproduced in any manner whatsoever without the
written permission of the author.

First Paperback Edition

DEDICATION

This book is dedicated to William Hart

INTRODUCTION

Out of the Shadows and Into the Night

Lovecraft's *Fungi from Yuggoth*, that odd sequence of sonnets the significance and interpretation of which remains so elusive even today, has always had its admirers and therefore, inevitably, its imitators—just as it may itself be (at least in part) an imitation of Donald Wandrei's *Sonnets of the Midnight Hours*. Most of these have been content to use the idea of such a sequence to tell a story, or present a set of imagistic or impressionistic visions, in the manner of the original. Such, for instance, are Ann K. Schwader's *In the Yaddith Time* or Lin Carter's *Dreams from R'lyeh*.

To go further, and actually use the original text as inspiration, to even write a sequence founded upon these poems themselves, requires an audacity almost amounting to *hubris*. To pull such a thing off, to avoid being *merely* an imitator, a *pasticheur*, to write what amounts to a gloss or, it may be, a pa-

Some Unknown Gulf of Night

limpsest, which obscures at the same time it evokes the original, while still remaining an original, personal vision of its own, requires genius of a rare order. Yet such is the essence of this book.

Wilum H. Pugmire has for some decades been an admirer, imitator, and *pasticheur* of Lovecraft. In his earliest work, that last was the most fitting description, as was also the case with the early work of Ramsey Campbell (of *The Inhabitant of the Lake and Less Welcome Tenants* period). Yet, like Campbell, even in those earliest works, something of Pugmire's originality was already peeping forth from behind the "eldritch blasphemies" of overt imitation of what many perceive as the style of H. P. Lovecraft. Relatively quickly—though at a slower pace than perhaps he would have liked—Pugmire, like Campbell, began to abandon this easiest and least substantial form of flattery for that of the underlying vision of Lovecraft's bleak yet wondrous universe. In his creation of Sesqua Valley—taken up in deliberate emulation of his mentor's creation of "Arkham Country"—he conversely took yet another major step toward independence; for, while owing its inspiration (a particularly apt word given the atmosphere of the locale) to the Providence writer's haunted New England, the Valley is distinctly its own self; kith and kindred, but with an uneasy, at times even aggressive, familial difference, one which includes a sardonic lack of deference as embodied in the character of Simon Gregory Williams, the Beast of Sesqua Valley... until forced to show such by the malignly amused force of its elder. In recent years, he has moved even beyond this, to an admirer who, while paying *homage* to and drawing inspiration from his "God of Fiction", has created a body of work manifestly his own.

In this, too, he has followed the same path Lovecraft (and, to a degree, Poe before him) trod; while still wearing his influences openly—those familiar with Lovecraft not only through the fiction but the letters and poems; as well as with Poe, Chambers, Wilde, Smith, and Campbell, will no doubt recognize many of them here—he has nonetheless assimilated and transmuted them into a vision, a worldview, unique to himself. His nods to the writings he loves are no longer imitation, but *adaptation*; a drawing together of disparate elements into a quite different and personal other; a something with its own life, its own pulse... and its own dreams.

It is here, perhaps, that this sequence of prose-poems and vignettes has its closest kinship with the *Fungi*; for much of it, too, emerged from the dreams—sleeping or waking—of its author, and it represents in potent form that unique distillation just spoken of. For here, those elements taken from those sources—the rotting quays; the twisted towers of books; the pallid mask and yellow robes; the licking of the palms which themselves serve as mouths, eloquent and sensual, or even overtly sexual; the bells of the ghoul-infested spires; and countless others—all have taken on a disturbingly enticing symbolism belonging to Pugmire alone; imbued with a resonance which at times recalls, though it seldom echoes, the source from which it is drawn.

There is more, however, than this. As stated above, those who have read the writers listed, as well as others who either influenced or were influenced by H. P. Lovecraft, will recognize much here that is familiar. But it is not the same; nor does it—save on occasion—bear the same significance. It has been "seen through new eyes", revivified, recreated, much in the same fashion as the pre-Raphaelites would re-create the myths, legends, and folklore from which they drew the substance for their art; and, like their art, as also mentioned, it provides a gloss on the originals which in turn stimulates the reader toward dreams of his or her own. As Lovecraft once said of Dunsany:

> To the truly imaginative he is a talisman and a key unlocking rich storehouses of dream and fragmentary memory; so that we may think of him not only as a poet, but as one who makes each reader a poet as well.

So, too, does W. H. Pugmire not only share his dreams but, by their often elusive, wistful, and hauntingly indefinite nature, he makes of each reader a dreamer as well. As dreams were so often the genesis of Lovecraft's *Fungi*, so these strange growths, coupled with dreams of his own, are the substance of the present work; and those dreams in turn have the quality, to the mind receptive to their beauty, terror, and pathos, of lodging in the reader's mind, evoking dreams from within the reader himself.

I mentioned the pre-Raphaelites just now, and the analogy is not an idle one; for Pugmire's work, like theirs, is heavily sensual, potent with a latent or at times manifest sexuality (as well as an awareness of the disturbing links between sex and death) which may seem alien to its Lovecraftian origins in the mind of many. We should recall, however, Lovecraft's own evolving views on such matters, and his praise of not only the French Decadents, but the work of such later, often sexually explicit, writers as Hanns Heinz Ewers, and artists such as Sidney H. Sime (see, for example, his frontispiece to Arthur Machen's *The House of Souls*) and Anthony Angarola (whose work he most likely encountered in the illustrations for Ben Hecht's novel, *The Kingdom of Evil*, which are at times bluntly sexual). While there is little doubt Lovecraft would not care for the focus on sexuality, there is good reason to suppose he would recognize it as artistically valid. In this, too, Pugmire shows both his difference from and insight into the views and work of his mentor.

    This is, of course, a book of prose-poems and vignettes; as such, it should not be taken at a single reading. As with Lovecraft's view of operatic technique—chiefly drawn from his response to Wagner—Pugmire has certain *leitmotifs* which recur throughout the work, and these run the risk of being repetitious given a hasty or careless reading. Yet, once again with reference to the *Fungi*, which also share this technique, when taken more slowly and thoughtfully, these touches add to the weaving of a connected narrative; connected not only in incidents of plot, but theme, symbol, and atmospheric tensity, as with each repetition they take on added layers of meaning which then reflect back on what has gone before. Thus the work rewards both care in a first reading, and periodic revisits with a fresh and maturer perspective. As his work in general has continued to grow, so this work in particular shows forth Pugmire's abilities at a sustained effort of dream and nightmare.

    As one who was privileged to watch the growth of this strange "dream-fungus" from its beginning, I

Some Unknown Gulf of Night

invite you all to follow this strange, unique dreamer as he guides you in a journey through Lovecraft's sonnet sequence as seen through his eyes. Yet one may find that, though the visage bears the stamp of Wilum Pugmire's weird and wondrous vision, behind that pallid mask you may find yourself facing a few dark beauties of your own.

    J. D. Worthington
      December, 2010

It was a place that smelled of olden days, time-swept into some distant era of night, haunted by an age-old odor of dust, of darkness and dead dreams. It was like some obscured realm half-lost in time, disjointed from the neoteric age, with ancient alleyways into which one feared to walk lest one would be beguiled by secret things. The stench of rotting quays built over stagnant tides washed to me on the chilly wind and made me anxious to find the hidden place I sought. It was a place that had been marked upon a curious map found in a ghastly book and accompanied by a faded photograph. I thought I had been familiar with the old town, but with the aid of this map I now explored a pocket of the place that had lain unexpected and unsought. I staggered through queer curls of fog and followed the spray of mist that was my frosty breath, then stopped beneath one elder curved lamp post to study the photo-

Some Unknown Gulf of Night

graph again beneath feeble light; and when I looked up again it huddled before me, like something that had leaked out of dream. I slowly approached the window with small panes and peered into the dusky place beyond. I could not comprehend the twisted pillars that rose from various places of the floor, almost reaching to the room's low ceiling. I gazed a little while, until my cloud of breath fogged the pane and thus concealed the scene.

I backed away from the blackened building, then spilled toward the narrow plank that was its door, a threshold that did not hesitate to let me in and closed behind me without sound or force. I could not ascertain the source of dim illumination that filled the crowded room, the soft old light that was easy on my eyes and seemed to charm my beating heart toward calm. The twisted pillars that I had detected from peering through the window proved to be piles of books stacked impossibly high and draped with filigree of spider web. A drowsy odor of wormy age wafted to me from the books thus piled, and for some moments I shut my eyes and listened to the silence of the place where I was its single tenant of blood and breath. Yet even with my eyelids closed I saw those twisted trees that were the piles of books, those balusters that seemed to hold the blanket of shadow that loomed above them; and as I watched them through closed eyes I saw them lean and twist still more, beguilingly, so that their movement coaxed my limbs to bend until one thumb pressed against the floor as the other touched a thing of smooth cool leather. I opened my eyes and beheld the book next to my hand, and when I allowed my hand to open the book I was confronted with curious symbols that might have been words. I tried to speak one alien word aloud, although my lips protested the effort; and yet my whisper seemed to float into the air, which echoed it beneath the wind that laughed against the outside window.

    I turned another leaf and found a second photograph that revealed the dim reflection of a woman who was attired in a gown that seemed familiar, a figure that disturbed me for reasons I did not understand. Placing the photograph inside my coat's inner pocket, I stood and peered about me. I was alone in the room, no seller in sight, and yet my imagination fancied that it could detect another presence in the room, someone whose low and subtle laughter sounded beneath the moaning wind outside the window. Suddenly I grew afraid, for in my fevered imagination I thought I saw the dark blanket above me sink a little lower and begin to churn. Perhaps the blackness meant to take the book away, and so I wrapped it inside my coat as laughter sounded once again, within or without I could not tell; and a burst of devilish wind thrust open the narrow plank that was a door toward which I flew until I found myself outside. I stood beneath the feeble light of an antique lamp post—beneath the sky of a calm, a windless night.

I kept the book beneath my coat and stepped into the quiet harbor street, walking through heavy coils of diseased fog that rose to meet the tendrils of black cloud with which they intertwined. I could not understand the curious shapes I seemed to see within the yellow fog, the flimsy faces lacking strength or substance that filtered toward me as if to kiss my visage with their melting mouths. A melancholy wail rose from the hidden harbor, perhaps the forlorn howling of some horn, perhaps the weeping of some lonesome beast. How curious that the faces in the fog curled their mouths as if in jollity. I could not understand the cruel laughter that echoed in the sickly yellow air. Staggering through evaporating things, I saw the outlines of tall and lean habitations that rose above and tilted o'er the lanes. I knew that this strange town was very old, and yet these habitations seemed to represent a fantastic past that did not wish to perish, of which these structures were an eidolon. Were they real and solid, the high and leaning things of brick and plank; or were they some freakish growth of elder memory that one may behold with eyes of lunacy? The hazy sight of them haunted my eyes and teased my buzzing brain with crazy hints, and I felt as though they watched me on my way with keen attention. Perhaps they knew that I had looked into the book, and thus my mind had been infected with occult residue. Perhaps if I placed my soft eyes against their planks and brick they would cool my buzzing brain with their cold surface, and I could rise, with them, above the harbor lane with tranquil peace of mind and watch the world in silence.

Thus compelled to kiss one antique wall, I crept toward the nearest dwelling and placed my mouth against a window pane. The vapor that was my mortal breath touched the glass as adhering cloud through which I peered into the place before me. I seemed to gaze into a haberdashery in which nebulous mannequins stood as still as stone, figures attired in unfathomable fashion that clung unwholesomely to their indefinite forms. Nearest to the pane through which I peered was a thing wrapped in yellow, tall and dominant and masked with a silken sheet that sheathed its dummy head. I breathed onto the glass as I looked in and hugged the secret book closer to my chest; and I wondered at the heavy beating of my heart, at how its palpitation echoed in the filthy air. When finally I brought forth the book from underneath my coat, my heartbeat seemed to sound within it, as if my pulsing organ had been coaxed inside. I opened the vibrating pages before the window and showed them to

Some Unknown Gulf of Night

the yellow mannequin as quiet laughter sounded in some obscure place (within me or without I could not tell). The figure behind the window raised a yellow talon and pressed it to the patch of my mortal vapor that still fogged the glass. A golden emblem formed beneath the moving finger, and I frowned as I tried to recollect where I had previously encountered the insignia. Something in its liquid shape disconcerted me, and thus repulsed I backed away as the yellow sign displaced itself from the window's surface and floated to the ground, where it floundered like some aquatic thing that had escaped its bowl.

    I fled the place and flew down darkened lanes through fog and shadow and harbor stench. The buildings watched my flight as I rushed past them, and I could almost detect the furtive faces that smiled at me behind the curtained windows. What kind of creatures hid within such dwellings? What secrets did they whisper in the dark? I sensed those rare whisperings pursue me, as if they hungered to nestle in my ear. Stumbling once, I dropped the arcane book, that tome that had captured the beating of my heart. It opened and heaved my heartbeat into the lightless aether. I bent and picked up the tome and clutched it to my quiet chest, as I—a heartless mutant—fled the haunted harbor lanes.

I staggered through the yellow fog, following the vibration of my heartbeat in the air, until I saw the house that grandfather had built when he was young, the place that I had inherited after father's death. It was there that I lived my little life in silence and solitude, where some few nights would find me in the dusky attic wherein grandfather's library had been stored. I was happy to see the clean black sky above my house, no fog or amber moonlight or winking stars. I gulped in air that was no longer tainted with necromancy or nightmare as I pushed open the little gate and advanced to the steps that I climbed to the solid porch. I paused for one small moment and listened for any sound that might have followed me from the unwholesome elder realm; but all that could be detected was the faint pulsing of my lonely heartbeat, a sound that seemed to bend the air nearest my mouth. Whispering a weird little song, I removed the book from underneath my coat and opened it, and I laughed

Some Unknown Gulf of Night

as my heartbeat fell again onto the pages which, quickly closing, trapped my mortal vibration once more inside the book. Pressing the book against my chest I said a little prayer, and as the words were whispered I sensed my heartbeat pass through the book and return once more inside my breast, where it frolicked with my blood.

My eyes were enchanted by the soft pale light behind the door's small rectangular window, and I leaned against that door so that my eyes touched the window's cool glass. Before me were the muted and familiar shadows of my home, the silhouettes of grandfather's antique furnishings. I saw the double doors that led into my library, the place where I often slept on a comfortable couch with the book that I had been reading on my chest. Ah, what dreams had been inspired in that place by the books that lined its shelves; and what dreams might blossom in my brain now, woven by the heavy book found in a foreboding shop. Contemplating this, I pressed against the door with that portal, the heavy book in folded arms, and as I leaned forward the door opened against my weight. As I stumbled forward, my large foot caught upon the doorframe, and in my attempt to catch my balance my arms flew outward and dropped the book, which opened as it fell before me and landed gently on the ground, caught by adoring shadow. I gazed onto the pages before me, at the ancient script and bewildering symbols, and ached to understand the esoteric lore revealed. Clutching the book, I carried it to the library doors, but when I looked inside the room it seemed too sane, its atmosphere too modern. Thus I climbed the steps that led upstairs and passed through the door that took me to the other steps that ushered me into the attic where grandfather had kept his library of ancient lore. I did not often enter this attic space because of the way in which it had been built. The walls and roof slanted slightly in curious ways, giving the room a queer irregular shape; and the air, inhaled, tasted dry and vaguely sour, so affecting my senses that I breathed in an unnatural manner. Electric light had not been installed in this portion of the house, and family tradition dictated that candles were to be the one source of illumination. I did not instantly light a candle because of the vintage tailor dummies that stood among the furniture and trunks and shelves of ancient books. The purpose of these mannequins was never explained to me, but something my father once said suggested that the feminine garb with which they were attired had belong to my grandmother, a woman I had never known. Thus they stood like forlorn eidolons, silent speakers of an unknown, unknowable, relationship.

Sitting at a centuried desk, I lit a candle and placed my hands on the weird old book that I had pilfered from the curious shop. It was fabulous, in an uncanny way, how the candleglow caressed the leather binding of the book, causing it to lighten from dim brown to dark yellow. Gazing at the thing I became aware again of the beating of my heart. I placed a protective hand inside my coat and pressed it against my chest, an action that reminded me of the photograph I had discovered between the leaves of the archaic tome. Slipping it out, I studied the faded creature pictured thereon, a woman whose face was a feminine copy of mine own, whose sen-

Some Unknown Gulf of Night

sual body wore a gown that I had seen before. Lifting my head, I scanned the room and beheld the tailor's dummy attired in an amber evening dress, and I marveled at the way the attic room's flickering light played upon the golden broach pinned to the gown. I floated to the mannequin and touched my hand to the smooth antique fabric of its attire as an aura of pale shadow encased the thing and me. Lifting the hem, I pushed myself beneath its yellow folds and kissed the sleek black wood of one of the three supporting legs of the dummy. Lifting higher, I ran my tongue along the rough surface of the feminine trunk as my hands scrambled to the twin mounds that were its imitation breasts. I stood and turned around as the gown fitted over and embraced my body.

The ancient book was before me. Touching it, I pressed the pages to my heaving bosom as some outside thing shook the attic window with faint fumbling. I watched the small window open and tasted the different air that rushed toward us and played with the frocks of my sisters. A breath of wind took hold of my photograph and lured it to and out of the attic window, and reaching for my flat and latent image my hand became elastic and spread toward outer darkness. Holding tightly to my book, I drifted through the window, into night.

We rise as smoke, my sisters and myself. We curl around the altar that has called us. We relish the weird old language, however inadequately it has been spoken by your mortal tongue. Now reawakened, we will teach your tongue correct enunciation in time of dreaming. We whirl around the dank stone of an altar that rises from some small pool of unclean water; we whisper at the thirsty things that flow to feast upon the pool's squalid nourishment, those beasts who ape the shapes of men as they spit madness into your mortal realm. The day has come at last, when the child-like thing that huddles in the hollow of an olden oak will dig its claws into the rank herbage on which it grazes and wraps itself in moist and filthy roots as it whispers predictions into the starlit vault of sky. Aching to feed upon its apocalyptic murmuring, we conjoin (my sisters and myself) as one entity and filter to the hollow of an elder oak. We twine the moist vines and leaves that cling to bark into our phantom hair and blend our

Some Unknown Gulf of Night

spectral blood with pus and pulp. We chortle as the child-like thing speaks the name of a strange, grey world with such precision that the air nearest its mouth thickens with chilly darkness. We love the cold dead world past the starry void, Yuggoth and its fungi. We long to dwell within its pockets and its pits, to flow beneath antediluvian bridges as substance in the swift black rivers on which the ghastly light of a daemonic moon sneers.

And now the child-like thing seeps from its hollow in the primordial oak, to stretch its pale white body toward the altar that rises from a stagnant pool. We creep below it as its black shadow as a groundmist, rising, chokes your mortal mouth. We weep with pleasure as the child-like thing dips its lips into the pool of distasteful water and, rising, turns its coy countenance to you. We love the fear reflected in your mortal eye, the fear that wears a taint of beguilement as the child-like thing seeps toward you, to your mouth, and drools its monstrous language into your maw. And now it is our turn. We rise as smoke and becloud your eyes; your nostrils suck us in so that we may frolic with your brain. We teach you how to shut your eye and dream, and in your dream we teach you how to utter our rare language to the audient void. We swim to your roots of hair and flow out of your dome as strands of fungi that wave in rising wind. We teach you new appetite as the child-like thing spreads itself on dank altar stone and welcomes the ravishing of your mortal mouth.

Your mortal mouth is pale and undernourished, famished for a taste of nasty keep; and yet you still refuse to acknowledge this, as if such a disclosure would confess mental or emotional disability. So I remain silent as you read my newest tale in winter moonlight, as we sit on this tabletop tomb in an ancient burying ground where once Poe walked. How nervously you laugh when once my tale is perused, and I laugh as well, but my mirth is evoked by the nervousness reflected in your eyes.

"You've outdone yourself," is your feeble commentary on my work.

I exhale a cloud of breath into the frosty air. "Really? Do you mean you find it more outlandish than my last? That other one gave you such macabre dreams—such a wonderful compliment. To make you dream is my most earnest intent."

"Oh, you've inspired innumerable dreams," you sigh, bending to my bosom and kissing the flesh just above the bodice of my yellow evening gown. You keep your face near my flesh and drink in my

Some Unknown Gulf of Night

musky perfume. I lift my head and eye the myriad stars. "Let me take you home," you whisper, a daemon of desire. You lift your head and would gaze into my eyes, but I ignore you as I continue counting stars. "I would take you home and transport you to a place of which you have never dreamed," you promise.

I watch the black clouds that gather above us and, one by one, blot out the stars. I feel the sky-winds that spawn within those clouds fall to earth and comb my hair. You shiver at their kiss. "Your mortal dreams are so safe and sane," I mock. "But the dreams that I have sewn within your skull—ah, they are something novel."

You laugh, a paltry noise. "I couldn't understand them, your gift of dreams. They made no sense. They showed me a pale and shadowy place that I thought was familiar, although I knew when waking it was a place I had never seen in reality. I walked its roads, past domes and towers. I heard the distant pounding of some sea, the sound of which seemed to herald an impending fate. I entered a cemetery above the sea not unlike this one we haunt, and sat on a chilly slab, as we sit now. I could feel the age of that stone slab rise into my flesh and claim a portion of my essence. As I sat I saw a multitude of fireflies that congregated near the ancient church—that congregated and transformed into one solid form, a figure in a yellow gown, masked, who filtered to me through midnight air. She wore a yellow mask, and something in its features enthralled me, so that I hungered to kiss its silken surface. Just as, now, I hunger to kiss your face."

W. H. Pugmire

Your mouth is near my own, and I can smell your rancid mortal breath. I have had enough of this charade. I take your face into my hands and gaze into your eyes so that you can at last behold the stars that wink within mine own. I exhale a black cloud of uncanny breath that encases your startled visage, and then I remove my hands from your face and bring them to my own. I lift my mortal mask and thus reveal the black gulf that is my nature—and your destiny. "Let me take you home," I tease, as—full of jest—I suck you into my unfathomable void.

The wrack had been washed upon the rocks during the dark hours, and they were puzzled by its dilapidated state, for the night had been serene. It was not uncommon for vessels to wash ashore near northern Kingsport, but they sensed that this was different; for it was unlike any craft they had seen, exuding an aura of strangeness and decrepitude. The thing was a small three-mast schooner, such as had been used in carrying cargo from distant lands; but something in its configuration was all wrong, its angles and contours did not, in places, make sense. And when they advanced to climb on it, something in its reek of rotted wood caused unsettling sickness to churn stomachs and cloud minds. They did not like the way the shredded remnants of sail moved in the gentle sea-breeze, or the way the disintegrating ropes twined around black and splintered poles. They did not like the way the shadows of the hollow northern cliffs played on the undulating waves that pushed against the structure like greedy things that would devour all.

W. H. Pugmire

It was the poet among the watchers who stepped below and searched the cramped cabin for any written log, for poets are not afraid to dream the dark dreams or taste the kiss of uncanny fear; but everything that he looked on was deteriorated—except the small black galley table lantern with plain glass sides and a metal top that was decorated with star-shaped holes. The remnant of a squat black candle was still inside the thing, and the poet thought it might be useful on the dark cold nights he spent reading in his attic room, and so he took it and brought it up into the outer air. The soft daylight revealed the curious scratches on the glass sides that looked like esoteric signals that might have been formed by etching with knife or diamond. The others to whom he showed the lantern did not like the way the daylight played on the surface of the thing's black iron, but he dismissed their discomfort to the effect of the mysterious craft and its aura of weirdness. This was Kingsport, and they who lived here had become attuned to extraordinary things and curious ways. And so he took the lantern home and found a place for it on a stand near his reading chair in the attic room to which he escaped at close of day. He sat in his comfortable chair and did a bit of work on a poem that had proven difficult, scribbling by candlelight as night wind whispered at the attic window. In time he set aside his pen and pad and extinguished the candles in their crystal holders. The darkness in which he sat was comfortable, and yet he could not quite relax because his eyes kept returning to the lantern on the table at his side; and so at last he struck a tapered match to his antique oriental flint box in which he kept opium and put its tiny flame to the candle inside the small black lantern. The little light that spread on the candle's wick played with shapes and shadows on the attic walls, and the poet frowned in incomprehension—for what contents within his little room could cast such outré forms on wooded surface, silhouettes of domes and towers and malformed bridges that crossed deep caverns? Why did the walls of his attic chamber seem to tilt and slant, and of what did that remind him?

The poet shut his eyes and began to sing impromptu verse that gave form to the outlandish phantasy in which he found himself. And wasn't it odd, how he could suddenly hear the solemn bells of buoys from the distant harbor; and wasn't it weird, how near they sounded? He stopped his song and opened his eyes, and did not understand why the room looked so utterly unfamiliar; and then he realized that he was not in his attic chamber at all, but had somehow returned to the small dark cabin of the wrack, the antique lantern sitting on a crate beside him and casting a diagram of stars on the slanting walls. He noticed the small oriental metal box on the floor, similar in style to his antique flint box, and he reached for it and unclasped the lid. Inside was the withered debris of age-old tea, and dry as the stuff appeared, still the poet could detect a slight aroma. Closing the lid and pocketing the container, he reached for the lantern and vacated the cabin with its crazy walls and slanted ceiling. Sharp moonlight mingled its dead illumination with the lantern's living flame. The ruined craft was still nestled on an outcropping of rocks, and yet one portion of it was in water that gently rocked it. Cautiously stepping to that portion still in water, the poet held his lantern outward and peered into the place below the surface; and he could not understand why the water seemed so deep so near to shore, nor could he comprehend the yellow thing that watched him beneath black water. Gazing at it steadfastly, he determined that it was a large figurehead that had fallen from some ship's prow. How its contours seemed to flow below the surface, so that the gigantic breasts encased in their yellow bodice seemed to heave. And the massive hand of one uplifted arm seemed to turn in circles; and as it circulated, the stars reflecting on black water moved with it, churning before his captivated eyes and summoning him to join in their danse.

He backed away and, holding the old lantern before him, found his way off the craft onto the slippery rocks, and then to the road that took him homeward. When once more he climbed the steps that reached into his attic room, the poet was comforted to see that it had regained its regular shape. Sighing, he placed the lantern onto its table, closed his eyes and sang himself to sleep. It was some slight sound that reawakened him, one that he could not identify. The squat candle in the lantern had burned low and was nearly gone. Becoming aware of a weight in his coat pocket, the poet brought forth the oriental container that he had found aboard the craft. The wee nap had reinvigorated him, and he felt a keen desire to return to working on his ode. Rising, he went to one corner of the room where he had a single electric burner with which he heated water for his tea. There was water in the kettle still, and so he switched on the burner and prepared his

Some Unknown Gulf of Night

cup and strainer. Opening the antique container he had found, he spooned out a small amount of the desiccated substance and spilled it into the strainer as the kettle sounded its banshee wail. Switching off the burner, he carefully lifted the kettle and poured hot liquid into the strainer. Clean water darkened as it filtered through the alien tea leaves. An aroma rose with the steam that sought his nostrils, pungent and full of promise. Resisting his natural inclination to pour sugar into the brew, he set the strainer onto a small dish and brought the china cup to his mouth.

He gasped and gagged. He dropped the cup and saw it shatter on the wooden floor, and then he watched the dark steaming liquid that spread upon the planks and crept toward him like rapacious shadow. He gasped again and could not understand why the aether seemed so heavy and bitter. Again there came the noise that had pulled him out of dreamless slumber, the sound of wind fumbling at the attic window. Gazing again at the pool of spilled liquid, he watched the wisp of smoke that rose from it and shaped itself outlandishly as its tendrils wound to him through the air. His eyesight began to blur. There came again the sound of windstorm shaking the attic window, and the idea of gulping in that breath of nature so enticed him that he rushed to the small window, opened it and pushed his head and torso into night.

There was no wind, but there was night certainly. Indeed, there was naught else but blackness illimitable. He could not see the walls of his house, or moonlit trees dancing in mild tempest. There was no moon, no countless winking stars. There was no earth. And then the poet detected movement in some distant place deep below, and as he peered into the void a shape formed and lifted to him. She was encased in a tattered yellow gown that was decorated with filigree of seaweed, and he marveled at the splendor of her gigantic breasts that moved as she heaved a siren's song. She rose to him, through daemonic darkness, and the splintered lips of her chiseled countenance curled with sardonic ecstasy as, pressed to living flesh, they claimed the poet with their kiss.

No, do not offer me your white hand and try to hold me back. I do not feel your paltry fear. I am a poet, and poets relish velvet shadow and its secret kiss. Why else would I live in this old valley town, haunted as it is by mystic history? No, take away your hand and let me walk down the road that hies me to the great hill. Ah, you follow, do you? Then make no mortal sound, for I relish the supernatural hush of this spectral hour. Look at the late afternoon sky and the scene before us, looking so like that painting by the American Modernist, Albert Bloch, his 1938 piece entitled "Rutted Road." Look, there is the stone wall at our left, and the forlorn farmhouse with its spiral of smoke reaching for the misty grey-blue sky. Here and there stand the isolated trees naked of foliage, some living and some deceased. Another wall begins on our right-hand side, an ancient thing composed of rough-hewn stone much darker than the bleached rocks with which the farmer's wall has been constructed. It contains a curious... aura...doesn't it, this centuried wall that stretches before us into the place where mist thickens into fog? And there, half-hidden by the fog: Zaman's Hill, the forbidden place, with its dome rising to meet the gathering darkness of early nightfall. Listen, do you hear it, the cry of crow? There it flies, over us and toward the blanketed hilltop, our psychopomp escorting us to another realm, where we will dine on occult things. Ah, there is your white hand again; but this time it seeks comfort of companionship, so as to alleviate your fear. Let me wrap my black fingers around it as, together, we trod across this esplanade toward the haunted hill.

There, the clean white steeple of your god. Do you wish to step inside and grovel on your knees? Or shall we continue on our way, through this blanket of fog and up the tall and wooded hill, where perhaps we can encounter other deity to whom we can whisper lamentations? Come then, and climb, and thus approach the level where wind begins to whisper two centuries of secrets. Look there, our psychopomp the crow, dead and mangled on this green and wooded plot; but still it guides, with the wing that is unbroken and points upward to the place that has summoned. How like a lost boy you look, with your wide eyes and pale mouth. I shall tighten my hold on your white hand and lure you upward, to the place that awaits your mortal foot. The path grows steep and the fog begins to thin as we reach the end of woodland and emerge into a time of newborn twilight. Look there, my child, below us—see the muted lights of human habitation through the churning mist. How far away humanity seems now, from this place that we have reached near the crest of a great hill. Forget that paltry light of human habitation, for there beyond us is another

Some Unknown Gulf of Night

illumination, phosphorescent and unearthly, kissed by lunar radiance that shines down upon the ruins before us. Your hand is in my own, do not hold back; turn your eyes away from that vale of mortal memory. Press your foot upon the path that leads us to the place of buried lore and ghastly ceremony.

Smell the wind that brings the stench of Dunwich, two miles hence, and watch that wind frolic with my abundance of red hair. Smell the rot of some madness out of time that would split dimension and spill onto our eyes. What wonders would our eyes then perceive! Feel the cold moonlight that would drown us with keen lunacy! Help me free myself from this bodice of my yellow gown, rip it with your hot white hands. Allow my manumitted tits, no longer slaves of modesty, to point their nipples to the moon. Nestle your white face between my breasts as your savage hands continue their destruction of my dress, then sink onto your knees and worship the moist aroma of my sex. Kiss me there with your prosaic mouth, but do not work your phallus yet—you must remain a virgin one moment more.

Take my black hand, child, do not hold back. Let me lead you to the altar stone where dull dead stains remember when they were new and moist and darkly crimson. Kneel here, with me, before this altar on Zaman's Hill, in this place of ruin and remorse. Let me embrace you with my black arms as my dark mouth sighs whispers into that cavity, your ear. The wind continues to move and moan and pitch my length of hair so as to blanket your frail white mortality. Rise and moan with me, upon this altar stone; let me straddle you and rip my nails into your pale white flesh. Ah, how your wet red liquid fuels my appetite as it coats this altar stone. Yes, let it lift, my child, your aching phallus, plunge it deep within me as we ride the night-wind with ghoulish delight. Let my rich red hair blanket you as I ravage what remains of your soul. Pump and pant, my pet. Part your paltry human lips and gasp in pain as the hill explodes with wondrous sound. Watch with gluttonous eyes the blood that floods the lunatic moon, the moon that illuminates my charnel hunger—my jaws stretched wide.

VIII

He had climbed the hill from which he could look down and study the ghostly seaport that had such a strange underground legend. One could well understand the whispers told of shadowed Innsmouth, for from this high point it looked like a huddled haunt in which nothing had dwelt for decades. The sunset had been spectacular, but as twilight approached he saw that there were no lights twinkling in the old town, which spread below like some lightless necropolis. The only movement was that of waves, of the sea that shook what remained of the rotting wharves, and the movement of thickened shadow as daylight died. At last he picked up his bicycle and rode down the trail that took him to the harbor, where the ancient winds brought evil smells from the sea and mingled with the sickening stench of Innsmouth town. The rain, when it began to fall, chilled his flesh but did nothing to dissipate the odor of sea and dilapidation, and so he continued his trek to the center of town, where he found, at last, the darkened shop that was his destination. Leaning his bike beside the weathered wall, he wiped away the rain that streamed into his eyes and peered through the murky glass; but all that he could discern was a tenebrous realm filled with curious forms, with here and there twisting columns that threatened to tilt and collapse. Bending away from the window, he raised his face to the rainfall and drank an effluvium of tainted sky, and then he stepped to the narrow door and entered the shop, instantly beguiled by how the air was altered, how his nostrils were pleased with age-old fragrance that dispelled the grotesque stench he had encountered outside. It was subtle, this new aroma, but he thought he could detect a variety of spices, plus the distinct smell of olden books. It was the smell of books that reminded him of his mission.

An abstruse source of illumination came from one corner of the room, and when he walked toward it he saw what looked like a very old lantern that sat on a glass case, its circle of easy light not filtering beyond that particular corner of the room. He walked past the twisted pillars that proved to be columns of piled books reaching to the low ceiling, from which decorative webs descended so as to cover antique lamps and items brought in from alien shores. His hands pushed away a tracery of dusty web from the glass of the case in which he beheld the book whose existence had been whispered to him in Arkham. Then he heard movement from a distant place, and looking up he saw the creature that stalked toward the circle of light. She entered the radiance, the tall black woman with lengthy coils of burnished red hair that hung to the waistline of her yellow gown. He was astounded at her handsomeness and won-

Some Unknown Gulf of Night

dered that a woman with skin so black was devoid of any sign of Negroid features. She seemed to him like some supernal goddess of Arabia who, although in mortal disguise, could not dissemble her cosmic sovereignty. There was something haughty and proud in her magnificent face, and he felt flattered when she deigned to smile at him and speak.

"What is your desire?"

"To look upon the sign."

Her smile altered, strangely, and her breath, as she pushed it to him, was filled with the intoxicating fragrance that he had detected upon entering the shop. "And what is the gift that will then be exposed?"

"I will know the Satanic glory of what it means to be a god." His voice was calm, but his hands, upon the glass of the display case, trembled. His eyes, bewitched, watched her reach into the case and bring forth the large book, from which another scent arose, one that he could not comprehend. Perhaps it was the effluvia of antediluvian sorcery, decayed yet potent still. He backed away a little as the smell reached into his nostrils and crept toward his brain, and then he blinked as his eyesight dimmed. Vaguely, he could see her delicate hands open the book. The golden symbol was blurred, but as he blinked his stinging eyes it took on solid form. It was a yellow sign, and it possessed him utterly. He watched with eyes on fire as the goddess curled her black fingers around the sentient glyph and raised it over her amazing face. He watched, enchanted, as the symbol's three tails mutated with shaping, until the thing became a triple crown composed of gold-white lava. He saw how its liquid light spilled over the place where the goddess had worn a magnificent face, but where there was now naught but a featureless mask of obsidian blankness.

Her hands, unaltered and amazing, reached for his face and tugged it to the triple crown. As he peered into its potency, he knew for one brief moment what it meant to be a god, a creature bereft of heart and soul, merciless and mighty. The beautiful hands brought his face nearer to one spire of the sign until his eye was pressed against it. Ah, how his eyes boiled and turned black as his flesh began to flake as ash. From someplace within the void that was her face, an orifice opened, and the goddess blew his dust away.

IX

Returning to the place that smelled of olden days, I staggered through the mortal throngs and sought the lonesome place, until I came to the leprous wharves that so infected my imagination. It was not only the coils of mist that rose from the water, but the sound of those waves as they slapped the rotting wood of dilapidated piers. It was a noise that felt like liquid footfalls on my brain, the tread of something trying to infiltrate my fevered fancy. From some distant indiscernible place I heard the baying of a vessel's horn, a noise so mutated by the aether that it sounded like some monstrous chanting to strange gods, and it was accompanied by the unhallowed gongs that were the clanging of moored buoys floating in some shoal. I walked away from the wharves and past the foreboding shop wherein I had found the ancient book, continuing to a network of alleys through which I hobbled, seeking the lonesome place that had been indicated on the curious map that I had found. Windowless walls tilted

W. H. Pugmire

over me, their roofs almost touching, and I felt covered by a canopy of rotted wood and displaced time. I kept my hands in pockets so as not to be tempted to touch the stagnant walls, wet with slime that caught and reflected darkness.

I saw it then, before me in a secret plot of land, the black courtyard that I sought. Edging through filthy shadow, I touched the cold metal of the gate, and then I pushed the gate and passed through the threshold. How queer that I expected someone to be awaiting me, from whose lips would be uttered the mysteries of the worm; but I was alone, and the one whispered sound that could be heard was the weird low song of wind in trees, and that was such a lonesome noise that, pursing my lips, I whistled in uneasy accompaniment. And then it was that a dim light illuminated the place before me, the moldy house of another era, where in one window I discerned an eerie glow. And from that window I heard a whistled sound that seemed to be an answer to my own, a noise that beckoned me forward, past a little pond in which glazed eyeballs seemed to study me. I approached the black wall and slanting roof from which diseased vegetation grew, and as I peered into the window I saw the dancing swarm of headless things that moved in time to song of wind and distant rhythmic buoys. I watched them raise their handless arms and slap their wrists together as they danced, and then I perceived the thing around which they moved, the gigantic yellow mask that fumbled on the floor, inching its way like some diseased worm as its black lips puckered and exhaled a ghastly chirrup of airy lamentation.

I tilted as I fell to weakened knees upon soft

Some Unknown Gulf of Night

ground and cried a call that seemed to inspire the dancing things to more feverish movement. The lifeless light behind them cast their horrid shadows on my brow, and I fancied I could feel their fantastic forms melt into my eyes and find my brain, into which they capered as arcane beasts eager to endow my mind with ceremonial task. I wept for the headless things because I knew that I would never taste their diabolic kisses, would never feel the trembling of their missing hands upon my face and in my hair. However, I felt the vibration of the yellow mask that had won their veneration, and I sensed its hunger to suck my boiling brain from out its dungeon, my smooth skull, to feast upon my head and hand so that I could join its throng of revelers. But I will not limp into that realm where human hope is démodé; for I have lips with which to breathe the arcane song that frolics in my mind, the tune that coaxes the yellow mask to lift into the air and float before my face, which it would eat. I still have hands, with fingers that are ripe for ripping and nails with which to shred a yellow mask and plant its tattered remnants into the necks where heads have been mercilessly severed. I watch them move as, now, the yellow moon reveals her face within the window of the room, and with language learned from arcane books I blend that lunar light with sentient shadow so as to construct artificial hands onto the severed wrists that writhe around me. They watch me, my adoring horde, with artificial faces as I move my hands in symbolic fashion to the dead lunar light, and they lift their dummy hands so as to impersonate mine own with movement that is reflecting on the surface of the moon.

W. H. Pugmire

We howl with wonder as the yellow moon assumes an expression that delights our morbid souls. I heave my whistled song into the air, accompanied by the things that whistle around me with those objects that have replaced their mortal mouths. They warble their puppet song into the cosmic darkness and dance in light of moon, remembering when they were living things. Nourished by necromancy, I join in their danse.

X

You lift your moody eyes toward the moon and watch her sepia half-mask slip askance and fall through cosmic aether to your face, to which, sensuously, it adheres. The sphere's dead antique light consumes your visage and is your only apparel. I guide our little boat to the middle of the black lake and drop my triple hook into its depths as your wind-swept wig conceals your derrière and laces the loins from which your phallus hangs. Your mask stops just beneath your nostrils and thus your cruel smile is evident as you whistle a song to which we once had waltzed. My triple hook grows weighty with its catch and I drag the long-buried item from the depths until its heavy fabric floats into my embrace as, clutching it, I pull it onto wood. Excited now, you point your prick toward shore, and I work the oars of our little boat until we are secured next to the landing. Whistling still, you waltz onto dry land and lift your heavy arms unto the moon, and then you bend your arms to me and take the soggy yellow gown from out my hands. I plant my faun-like hooves into the ground and allow my hands to nestle 'round hermaphroditic loins as you slip into the soggy yellow gown and call to daemon wind to dry your dress. It comes, in answer to your summoning, yet it is not alone. I cannot see the flowers at my feet, for smoke and shadow cloud my dull eyes; yet I can feel the soft flesh of a rose and smell the wilted lily's rank decay, and I can taste the realm from which humanity dreams and weeps, the place to which you lead me in the blithe motion of continued dance.

We reach the neglected area of town and enter the dusky theatre. We push through double doors and glide into the crimson auditorium, where rows of ruined pews reek of shredded leather and stale tears beneath the candlelight of chandelier. I peer toward the raised platform that serves as stage and observe the twisted faces of embalmed clowns whose marble eyes wink secrets to the rafters where bedraggled birds mutter to themselves. I watch you run and leap onto the stage and stretch your yellow gown with naked hands. I watch you curtsy to the zany stiffs as if to teach them some new skill by which they could reanimate their limbs and blow you kisses from their dummy mouths. Your lips, delicately pursed, exhale an airy song, to which the birds, above, respond. I hear the beating of their tattered wings and watch their molted feathers drift onto the stage. I see them wing their way to you and plant their beaks into the fabric of your mask, and smell the streams of blood that slip through the places where your mask is ripped and torn. Your whistling assumes a liquid sound as bubbles

Some Unknown Gulf of Night

of blood float from your lips toward the zanies that would admire you; and as those bubbles splash onto the charnel mouths the music you exhale is subtly accompanied with other whispered warbling, a pleasing sound from reanimated apertures of flesh to which the crazy birds flutter. I watch the dry flesh of the clownish faces fall away in pieces to the floor, yet still the whistling sounds through grinning jaws stretched wide on physiognomies of bone.

    I cannot stand as passive observer any longer, and so I leap onto the platform and frolic on the floor, rolling into mounds of molted down that clings to that which answers for my flesh. And you, majestic master, finally appear, to hover over me with your strange smile as devil birds crown the air above you and laugh with beaks that are wet and red. At last you fall onto your knees above my loins and let your liquid mouth bleed into my womb.

XI

We could hear the music, faint as it was, from our porch, and I confess I took a fancy to the sound. Thus I got on my bicycle and pedaled toward the meadow just off the Aylesbury pike where the road leads to Kingsport. This meadow has long been a place I like to visit because of the rugged megaliths that stand there—I like the way the wind sounds as it passes through their upper holes and hollows. You experience rare dreaming when you recline against those megaliths at dusk and watch the gulf of night deepen over you, like some abyss you might fall into as you step from star to star. It felt sweet to ride beneath those stars that night, nice and easy, no need to hurry, curious as I was concerning the muted music. The sky wasn't its usual black but rather a deep dark blue bruised with hints of purple, and the wind smelled especially aged as it pushed me on my way. I could just see the hazy silhouettes of the megaliths before me on the spread of meadow where nothing grew except tall dry grass, and although there was no moon that night the starlight

Some Unknown Gulf of Night

seemed especially bright and so I could easily make out the yellow caravan and dilapidated pickup truck parked some distance from the groupings of pillars. The music had stopped for just a while, but then it started up again, and I knew that it was someone playing an accordion, although no person was in view. My bicycle glided to where the caravan had been parked, and I wondered how its yellow paint could look so bright in such dim light. Here and there someone had painted black stars on the yellow surface; at least I think they were meant to be stars, even though my eyes had trouble focusing on their forms, which seemed to shift and change in a way you wouldn't notice unless you stared at them with steady eyes like mine. Staring at stars was a favorite pastime of my ken—we liked the way their bodies stretched pointed extensions in such a way that suggested living creatures in the sky. These black stars on the yellow caravan had a similar effect, never seeming still but always expanding and contracting, as if they were breathing.

I parked my bicycle and sauntered to the half-open door of the caravan, which looked as if it had once been part of a traveling carnival. The person inside added to this impression, for he was a tall fellow dressed as clown, with gigantic hands and ears and red rubber nose. Strands of hair escaped from underneath a bowler hat, and I thought it kind of strange the way that hair was identical in every way to the tall dry grass that sprouted in the meadow. The fellow's queerest feature, his eyes, were sunken inside black hollows in his head—you could just see something shining inside those pits, something that gleamed like polished coal. An antique accordion was in his huge hands, its keyboard all shining silver with patterns of embossed design, and the music that he played from it, although rhythmic, had a quality of sadness in its sound, kind of like the music played by a group of Jewish musicians that had given a recital at Miskatonic University when I was a student there. The clown fellow bobbed his head in time to music, and then he began to stamp one foot so that the entire caravan began to shake. I watched the puppets that were hanging inside large glass jars on a table near him, puppets with their rainbow-hued strings attached in some weird way to the lids of the jars so that the funny figures hung in midair inside their cells. I wondered at the fabric with which those puppets had been constructed; there was something disturbing in the way the light of the place reflected on their sickly bleached simulation of skin. Maybe that was just the way the light played on and through the texture of the glass with which the large jars had been manufactured.

Clown-man stopped his noise and lowered his accordion onto his lap, and then he tilted his head and shut his eyes in a manner of listening. I looked away from him and listened as well, to the low haunting sound of the wind whispering through the cavities of the standing stones. This was a sound that I was familiar with and one that I enjoyed. Indeed, when I was away for all those years, attending college in Arkham, I would sometimes hear this song of wind through ruins in my dreams, like a kind of summons that persuaded my return to Dunwich. I stayed away for eight years and obtained the finest education that I could, because it was my plan to leave Dunwich eventually and try to establish life

Some Unknown Gulf of Night

in some city, as was common for most elder sons of this wasted pocket of the globe who have tasted life outside the village by attending Miskatonic or Harvard. Once I returned home, however, I knew that I would never leave. I felt too close a kinship to the domed hills and their secret sounds, to the dismal sky and they who dwelt beyond its dimensions. I relished the occult history of two centuries, fantastic legends of sacrifice on Sentinel Hill and of strange forest presences that laughed mockingly beneath the ground. That forest has a kind of enchanting beauty that I've never seen anywhere else, a beauty that soothes the eyes that behold it as powerfully as it disturbs the mind. So I returned home with a fine education and many books, and I worked my parents' farm and wrote poetry in my quiet hours. I was treated, almost, as a kind of outsider because of my education, because of the way I spoke, because I was able to write and think in a manner that was unusual to the ignorant lot that makes up the village. This backward kind of mockery reached its height when a small collection of my poetry was published by a small outfit in Boston. No wonder that so many of those young men who had earned an education found it necessary to leave the land. I would never do so—the elements of Dunwich flowed within my streams of blood. But I understood too well the desire to flee ignorance and scorn, especially from fools who had never accomplished anything in life. But there were others in Dunwich village who subtly understood my ways and with whom I exchanged unspoken communication. I felt a similar kind of communion in that meadow and its quiet carnival caravan, where clown-man and I listened to the song of wind that sighed through the crevices of pillars and chuckled inside hollows that wind and elemental time had formed.

The zany spoke. "I like the way yon wind sounds. You don't get wind like that in the city. Cursed city corrupts everything, including nature. There the wind is just another noise competing with man-made squeals and bangs and groans. Here, the wind sounds as it has for most of time, a wonderful primordial lullaby. Come lad—let's go outdoors and taste the ageless effluvium."

There was a lilt to his voice that sounded foreign, although I couldn't place it. I didn't look at him again because of his lack of eyes, which affected my imagination to the point where I felt that if I peered into those pits too deeply I would get sucked into their black light. So instead I watched his shadow on the wooden floor next to the discarded accordion as he stood and stretched and hopped out of the doorway into the dry tall grass. I listened to his tread as he slithered through that grass like some cunning serpent, and I heard his hissing into the subtle wind. Not liking the way his puppets in their jars looked at me, with their sad appealing eyes, I rose calmly and stepped outside to where clown-man was gazing at the midnight sky and pretending to shoot at a star with finger and thumb poised as pistol. How peculiar that the star, as I watched it, suddenly extinguished. I felt my flesh grow cold as, laughing in a low manner, he stepped near me and pointed his finger to my heart and wiggled his thumb.

"I like your wee village," he whispered, "despite its smell. Actually, that stench is a part of its allure

Some Unknown Gulf of Night

for me—such an old, forgotten taint, like rank prehistoric alchemy." His large nose touched my hair and sniffed. "Aye, I smell it on you too, a hereditary thing, no doubt, that reaches into a place of deep old time and they who pulse within it. I can smell the abyss of another dimension and the daemonic concavities of ancient earth, those places that have captivated your kind, those realms that have caught your imagination and keep you home. How rare, such loyalty. Come nigh, let's dance and reawaken dreaming things!"

He looked so comical as he raised his large malformed red shoes and began to tread on the ground to some music in his mind that I began to laugh and tap my toe to imagined song. Then, winking at me, he produced an ancient-looking Pan pipe, slim and double-columned and bound with black twine, with a length of cord with which one could slip the instrument over one's head and wear it near the heart. Pressing the columns to his mouth, he began to play the tune that I had heard inside my mind, an ancestral tune that I seemed to remember from another era. He played a little while and then he stopped beside me and, removing the pipe from his lips, offered the instrument to me. One heavy arm caressed my shoulder.

"'Tis easily done, laddie. Here, take it in your small white hands, there ye go. Listen to this lovely foehn that wafts to us from the surrounding hills and let it teach you how to blow. There you be, press those pipes to your lips and call the ones who dream in death. What a scintillating sound, like sparks of noise bursting into aether!"

There was such persuasion in his voice that

W. H. Pugmire

I couldn't help but play the role of Daphnis to his Greek god, and then something very odd happened. In my imagination the world around me blurred and altered and the distant atmosphere all around me became reflective, as if I were encircled by a wall of glass. Clown-man's gloved hands, suddenly larger than before, frolicked over me, wiggling their fat fingers in time to my piped song, and my dancing limbs seemed to answer to the movement of his hands, as if I were the creature's animated manikin. As I danced, the wind among the standing stones became a howling mistral—at least I thought it was the wind that bellowed and pushed hot breath upon my eyes.

"Tell me, son of Dunwich, of the secrets you have dreamed. I've journeyed far to ascertain such knowledge."

His phrase, the title he bequeathed me, reminded me of my heritage and brought to mind my place. Whatever kind of creature this may have been, it was now in my familiar realm, with which I was intimate. "I can do better than merely tell you," I sang as I capered beneath his gigantic hands. "I can show you." My saying so subdued his alchemy so that his proportions returned to normal size and whatever of his essence had leached onto my mind was gone. I slipped the pipe's cord around my neck and let the instrument nestle at my breast.

Sneering condescendingly he replied, "You can shew me a madness out of time, the pulsing shadow of unearthly dimension? I have sought such things around this paltry globe, aye, and the things that I have peered upon have stolen sanity and sight—but, oh, their rich reward!"

Some Unknown Gulf of Night

Finding my feet, I ceased my jolly cavorting and stood quite still. "I can dip you into other realms, into an abysm of old time, the place where secrets mutter underneath the hills of Dunwich. I can give you that, if such you require."

He turned his head toward his dilapidated pick-up truck and thought. "I have misplaced my mortal eyes by peering into arcane darkness, and now darkness dwells within these hollow holes that once looked so innocently at the world. My shadows have appetites that I must satisfy. They itch to graze on occult things, to seep into the places where such revelation may be found. Take me, then, young lad, to this environ of mystic revelation. Let me fathom, if I may, its timeworn tale."

Easily escaped from his strange spell, I walked beside him to the vehicle and shut my eyes as he followed spoken directions to my abode. My kinfolk had retired and so no one followed as I led the clown-man into the depths of earth that composed our secret cellar. His malformed feet stalked that sod as his bulbous nostrils sucked the rancid air until he found the place of buried sorcery that held ancestral secrets of murder and mayhem. Excitedly, he leapt upon the circular timber that covered the ancient well, that plank that was still discolored by my uncle's blood from when he was young and foolish and moved the covering so as to sniff the tarnished drafts that siphoned sanity and sucked him into suicide. I was but a child at the time of his death and have no strong recollection of my uncle, but there have been times when, dreaming near the well, I have heard his hungry cry—or whatever it was that spoke to me from the depths. I heard as well the hacking of his ax with which he had tried to splinter the wooden slab, that slab that still contained deep slits caused by heavy blade. I smiled and laughed out loud as clown-man capered on the covering as his comical nostrils sensed the beast below. Prancing to him, I indicated that we might, together, remove the cover and thus expose the banished foetor of a concealed place. He was strong, the zany at my side, and easily lifted the heavy circular plank and pushed it from us. I had never had the strength or inclination to try and remove the covering on my own, and it beguiled me that the nauseating stench that lifted to us was exactly as I had dreamed it at those times when, disturbed with loneliness, I had come to nap beside the centuried well.

"Alas," I whispered, looking down into the well. "There are no rungs on which to climb into the depths. I thought there would be. Too bad, it would have been wonderful to let you down there, to let you listen intimately to the earth noises that have kept Dunwich slumber so uneasy. What revelations that dark place would reward your senses! Oh well."

"Nay, laddie," was my companion's gleeful reply. "I have tricks yet!" So saying he reached into the wide pocket of his ridiculous garb and pulled forth rainbow-hued lengths of rope, and how he could have kept such a lot of it in that pocket defied sane reason. Truly, he was a clever clown. "Now then, wee boy, wrap these ropes around my wrists and tie them snug. Good. Now, tangle these others around my ankles, there you go! Hold them securely, sirrah, as I climb into the well and work my way into its aperture. Nay, don't fret. I know a way to make myself as weightless as whispered sin. Here we go!"

Some Unknown Gulf of Night

He stood on the brick ridge and waved goodbye with comic exaggeration, and then he jumped into the tainted air. As he drifted downward his body seemed to shrink in size and lighten in weight, so that he seemed no more than a marionette for me to play with. Down he drifted, out of sight, but I could yet heed his ecstatic voice.

"*Gawd! If you could see what I am seeing with what is left of my ember-eyes! It's terrible—monstrous—beyond anything! So this is the secret of decayed and poisoned Dunwich! How can I describe it? Not with mundane language. It's too utterly beyond thought—and yet I ache to name it so that you too can feast upon its horror. But—but I think it knows you, for I seem to see your resemblance in the contours of its half-face! Is this the thing that calls to you in vision, the thing that stalks the stars? I have had visions of nameless horror, but I never dreamed of THIS!*"

"Wait!" I called down. "Let me teach you ritual danse, so that you can adore it as it so demands. There, see how I pull your strings and move your limbs. What? It has suddenly noticed you, the thing that murmurs and has appetite? You're afraid? What's that? The noises of the earth are like needles in your stretched ears? How jolly! Wait, I'll pull you up a little, so that you dangle in the malignant air, just like your puppets in their jars. What will happen when I return to your caravan and smash those jars with my uncle's ax? It will be a spectacle, I'm sure! Quick! Let me reach for the slab, which I pretended was too heavy for me, but look! I move it easily. Here, let me slip these ropes through the crevices in the wood, from which your howls echo just like the wind that whispers through those standing stones. Hang there, in mirthless solitude, and let your companion feast. *Bon appétit!*" So saying, I hurled myself onto the slab of circular wood and imitated the jester's dance, laughing at his tormented howls. And then I took hold of the pipes that still hung around my neck, brought them to my mouth, and performed a paean to the horrors of Dunwich.

XII

You meet her in the cold sunlight before her new unhappy home, and when she lifts her black veil for one momentary kiss, your heart breaks to see that she is merely a wizened spectre of the woman you once adored. Seeming to sense your unspoken critique, she drops the heavy veil over too-pale skin. Not one speck of flesh is exposed, she is wrapped entirely in black; and when at last she offers you her gloved hand and leads you down the pebbled path it is like walking beside a thing of sentient shadow, some midnight spook. Your awareness catches the murmurings that plague the sunlit air, yet you cannot ascertain if they issue from the windows above or the river below. You see the high fence that divides the ground and river bank, the fence that is meant to discourage those who dare from dancing into the water's current; and you smile wistfully at the memory of when, as child, you thought to sink into the river yourself and end the hideous thing called Life. Sensing your memory, she links her arm with yours and turns you away from water's movement. She leads you down the path of ruddy cobblestones where she tries not to notice the dark amorphous shapes that hide, tittering, behind low shrubs and bushes, below the boughs of lean and hungry trees; and yet something in the suggestive shapes she almost sees causes her to tremble, and so you secure your arms around her with hands that accidentally touch the dugs that, long ago, nourished your infant mouth. How hot her bosom feels to your cool hands.

The edifice into which you cannot enter spreads before you, red and white, and you try not to look at it. There, before you, is the inanimate fountain, as dry as your heart, that pumping organ that is too afraid to enter the building wherein your father perished. What is it that you fear? To smell the monstrous aftermath of madness that may yet taint the walls within? You do not dare to enter, and yet you allowed her sisters to send her there, where she wanders in her widow's weeds and listens to the beckoning river beneath the sloping stones. You cannot think on it, and so you whisper poetry into her ear as you watch the fading day, until at last you cannot ignore the faint howls that issue as from a room above on the second floor. And then the howling increases in intent, and the one beside you melts at the sound into a cloud of shadow that drifts from your embrace. You can no longer ignore the howler

Some Unknown Gulf of Night

from above, the one who screams your name. It is there, the thing on which your forlorn eyes must feast—the baying wretch that wears your mother's face.

XLII

    Two nymphs of evening danced around the apple tree of a sunset garden beyond the spires of mortality, two airy nymphs that she could see in dream alone when songs of fancy floated in her brain. She had walked the rustic path through woodland where the forests of the waking and the dreaming world just touch, and had consumed the witch-brewed potion that shut her eyes and spun filigree of vision, a web that caught her mortal pulse and beguiled her blood to spill toward the other realm. Ah, sweet sphere!, where chimneys detached from place of man spill perfumed smoke into the gulf of gathered night, smoke that copulates with clouds so as to spawn the creatures of the air. They peer, those daemons, on the lass who creeps toward the apple tree and admires its golden fruit. Two nymphs, their faces concealed beneath yellow masks, welcome the newcomer with graceful hands and motion to the hanging fruit. The lass of blood and sinew sees beyond the branches with golden fruit to the gnarled bough

Some Unknown Gulf of Night

on which one single apple hangs, a thing as black as deceptive nightmare. Her amber hand reaches for dark fruit and plucks it from the withered branch. Her eyes, beguiled, look onto the apple's flesh and see the points of infinitesimal light, like little stars within the core of night. The nymphs of evening move about her and the tree as she brings the apple to her jaws that tighten 'round its smooth warm skin. As she partakes a place within the gulf of night is anxiously consumed, a rip in heaven from which a red rain falls. The crimson liquid melts away the yellow masks and thus reveals the naked things beneath, the blood-hued hags who reach for their new sister. Three nymphs of nightmare dance around the dying apple tree.

XIV

I entered the city of mists on a day when the yellow sky was cool and clear, on an autumn day when dead leaves rushed around me and rose in whirling wind. Curls of chimney smoke mingled gracefully with autumn wind as I stepped down hilltop streets into the winding lanes of what seemed the main section of Kingsport. Stopping at one shop, I purchased a warm green scarf, for it was my fancy to sleep beneath the abyss of night. My walking tour of New England had been a wonderful experience, and although I had been a wayfarer for many hours I was not yet worn out. Studying my street map, I followed the winding lane that took me to the hillside burying ground. I climbed the steps that led to a sturdy bench, where I could sit and watch the yellow sky grow pale, then purple. I looked down the sloping hill, past tombstones black with age, over the rooftops to the harbor. I knew that somewhere below was the haunted place that I sought, and taking the book out of my knapsack, I opened it to where I

Some Unknown Gulf of Night

had placed a hand-made map given me by an acquaintance who had lingered in this town for three years. It was the book, actually, that had brought me to this mist-shrouded seaport—the slim volume of macabre verse by Winfield Scot. I came to Kingsport because I was obsessed with my dark dreams, and Scot's book of poetry was a collection of his cosmic nightmares put to rhyme—and some of them seemed damnably familiar. The artist who had introduced me to the poet's work had been a part of Kingsport's transient community of artists, mostly students who had heard beguiling tales of the old town and came to seek mystic inspiration. Her stories regarding the mysterious poet did not make him sound very interesting; rather, she described him as a burned-out failure who lived like a street urchin and was over fond of alcohol. I listened to her tales with more interest than was evident—for she lacked the intimate connection of shared nightmare, and was herself a rather blasé soul. She had loved the old seaport, however, and was intimate with its lanes, and so I thanked her when she made me an impromptu map that indicated where I might find the residence that the poet claimed as home.

    I descended steps that took me to the road below, book and map in hand, and followed the handwritten directions as the sky darkened over me. A chill crept into the air, and so I wrapped my new scarf tighter around my neck as I approached the lonesome place that was the residence I sought. Walking past the queer-looking iron fence, I entered a pathway of wooden planks that led past tall yellow grass in which a series of painted stones had been curiously grouped, reminding me of pictures I had seen of mysterious megaliths, although the things I passed as I tramped along the wooden walkway were diminutive in size compared to the massive tombs in Ireland or other famous standing stones. There was something in the way the stones were grouped that made me think of secret things, and this inspired me to quiet my tread and walk as silently as possible toward the crazily slumped and tilted house ahead. Hearing a night bird's cry, I turned to look behind me, at the darkening sea from which a mist began to rise. Then I continued my way to the porch, where a fellow sat and read by lantern light.

"Are you lost?" a slurred voice asked as I noticed the bottle of whiskey beside the fellow. The antique lantern's light was bright enough to illuminate his face, and I was surprised to find the chap so young-looking. I judged him to be around thirty-three years of age. I was disappointed in his dullard face, which seemed completely lacking in intelligence of any kind. Could this be the visage of the poet whom I sought, this tramp with dark disordered hair and dim expression in his slightly slanted eyes? His dusky flesh suggested a mixture of foreign blood, and his large Kafkaesque ears made me suspect he was, in part, Semitic. Something in the intoxicated bleary eyes disturbed me—I sensed that they might be some kind of camouflage concealing a persona that was not as dim-witted as he appeared. They contained a kind of surreptitious knowing that only an intelligence as keen as my own might detect. Not knowing what to say, I merely mumbled some lines of verse that I had memorized from the book. His eyes darkened as his listened to my chanting of his poesy, and then he laughed and lifted the bottle to his lips.

I brought forth my hand that held his book. "I admire your work," I mumbled. "I want to ask about your dreams."

He clapped his hands once and held them to me. "Toss it here. Damn, I haven't seen a copy since I don't know when. I don't remember it being so slim."

"It's captivating work," I said, not moving as he thumbed through the book that I had thrown to him.

"Is it? I was very young when I wrote this stuff, a mere child. People reacted like I was some kind of prodigy, those who weren't freaked out by the nature of the work." Reminiscently, he smiled. "I preferred the ones who were disturbed—that seemed the more genuine tribute to my visions. Queer thing is that as soon as the book was published my dreaming ceased—poof, gone. I was a ten-day wonder, and then the sun had set on my talent and temporary fame. So I left home and began to wander, trying to find those places that might inspire new dementia. Hell, the world is a prosaic place. Luckily, I drifted into Kingsport and found another dreamer, an ancient sea captain who could spin a tale that would set my imagination on fire. Damn, he inspired me, and the poetry poured forth once more." He must have noticed the excitement in my eyes, for he shook his head and laughed again.

W. H. Pugmire

"Nope, never published. It's all in there, on yellowing sheets that have never seen the light of day." He jerked his thumb toward the door of the dilapidated cottage, and then his voice became a whispered sound. "But you don't want to go in there. Catch." He tossed the book to me. "Why do you seek me? You're not a poet."

"No—I'm a dreamer." A distant church bell tolled, and Winfield Scot sighed. "I've seen things that reminded me of your poems. I've heard strange music piped by amorphous *things* that squatted before a throne of fire, music that was accompanied by the groaning of cosmic wind that fell from starlight. You've heard this to, if your poetry is to be believed. Tell me what it means."

He suddenly stood and staggered drunkenly down the wooden walkway and onto the grassy place where the tall stones stood. Turning to gaze at me, he leaned onto the tallest stone, an oddly-painted thing that resembled the Eye Idols excavated by Agatha Christie's husband in Tell Brak in 1937. Joining him, I touched my finger to the idol and found its stone peculiarly soft. Scot ignored me and scanned the sky with sober eyes. "Don't you get it, friend? There is no meaning. Nothing matters. We stumble with our paltry illusions on this tiny sphere of dust and then we die." He shrugged. "It doesn't matter. We have experienced life, which is its own hellish reward. The safest existence is the one that's impotent. I am a beast of nothingness. It suits me fine. Fuck, don't look so dashed."

My hollow laughter floated out my mouth. "That's exactly how I feel, dashed on the rocks. And

Some Unknown Gulf of Night

I thought you might have taught me how to step among the stars."

Roguishly, he cocked his head. "That's the easiest thing in the world." Stepping to me, Scot placed his arm around my shoulder and led me out of the yard, down the road and to the shore. We listened to the gentle tide and watched the dark water, now free of evening mist. A blanket of shimmering starlight was reflected on the surface of the sea. "There you go," he sang.

I gazed out to the reflected stars and felt a wind drift to me from the water. Or was it a star-wind that would coax me forward, into an abyss? The more I looked outward, the more beautiful the sight became. "Will you come with me?"

He shook his head. "Nah. Not now. Perhaps in time. I am still a moonstruck poet, you see, and although my pen has stopped I still have lips with which to utter poesy to the spheres. I still have dreams, in which I feast on fungi sprouting on distant Yuggoth, wherein I sense the perfume of undreamt continents beneath alien moons. I stepped through earthly gardens, seduced by perfumed winds just as sweet as any cosmic nectar from a fallen star. I have Kingsport, a realm unto itself, as perfect as the strangest dream. I need no other place or time."

I offered him his book of verse, which he refused—but as he backed away from me he sang a snatch of verse:

"The midnight constellation calls my face
As I stargaze into eternity
Wherein I find a more congenial pace

W. H. Pugmire

Undreamt of by dim, dull humanity.
Far from mortal days I ache to soar,
Far from flesh, this squalid weight of mud
That forms this prison-husk I so abhor,
This useless husk of skin, of bone and blood."

I heard them call above and beyond me, the shifting stars that swam the sky and were reflected on the water. Clutching the book of poetry to my chest, I moved into the water and walked the spaces between the stars. As I moved, my weight altered, as if I might surrender it and freely float into the dark abyss. I was submerged, but by water or black welkin I could not ascertain. And although other things, shapeless and soundless, floated by me, I had never felt so utterly alone. I opened my mouth and drank the liquid fire of a star, and thus my vocal chords were so transformed that I could chant poetry as never before. A strong current (of water or of air I did not know) seized Scot's book from my hand and I watched it drift and disappear into the audient void. It did not matter, for the verse lived within me and danced upon my tongue. I opened my mouth with music and sang the liturgy of nothingness.

XV

It rose before them on the apex of a snow-covered hill, like an object found in deep dreaming, the ruined edifice with its three towering pillars. Something in its circular shape reminded the woman of an artifact that she had seen in a museum at Miskatonic University, of an outré triple crown. Peering at the ruins so intently had a curious effect on Josephine Broers, for she imagined that she could see some queer winged shape perched atop one of the three columns; but then the thing fluctuated, separated and drifted away as dark cloud. She watched as Matteo marched before her, through deep snow up the precipitous hill, and after a slight uncertain pause she followed him, struggling through the snow as they climbed together toward the lonesome place. They had been prepared for the severity of weather, and they knew that the region was a place of uncanny legend; and yet they had not premeditated the psychological effect that confronting the ruins with naked eye would cast on them. Thus, mingled with the discomfort of deep snow and icy air was a sensation of almost primordial terror, some ancestral and psychological warning bell that could be felt in blood and bone. What overwhelmed Josephine was a feeling that they were utterly alone, in a place of unfathomable isolation.

Completing their arduous trek, they stood before the mammoth ruins and trembled—and they were uncertain what it was that caused their bones to shake and their hearts to shrink, the coldness in the air that grew more definite, or the indefinite alienness of the ruins before them. The thing looked prehistoric, and the place was so shunned by neighboring localities that there were no legends concerning its origin or race. It was a place that had existed since primordial time, epochal in a way that could be intuited if not comprehended. What Josephine sensed was more than presentiment—it was like a deeply buried racial memory that had been shocked into wakefulness by the sucking in of the chilly aura all around them. The ruins before them stood like some defacement out of time, a thing that should not be—or should no longer exist. She watched as Matteo, much smaller than herself, stepped through the snow into the circular place wherein the tremendous statue crouched upon its monument. Josephine did not want to approach the thing, for the workmanship that had created it had been monstrously exact. She thought, initially, that it had been created from dark brass of incredible age; but now she suspected that the enormous statue had been chiseled by expert hands (or that which answered for hands) from a gigantic piece of black jade. It was in form an exact replica of the amulet that Matteo had shown

Some Unknown Gulf of Night

her on the night that he had convinced her to journey with him on this trek, the amulet of a crouched hound or sphinx that wore a semi-human yet daemoniacal face. She knew that the young man was wearing that amulet on this journey, although he was careful to keep it hidden from view.

She looked again at the grotesque statue and noticed one peculiar thing—it was naked of snow, whereas all other objects had been coated with inches of the stuff. At last she followed her companion to where he stood brushing snowfall from an idol that stood in a row with others. She marveled at the look of wonder in the young man's eyes. "It's the Seven Dreamers! I can't believe it. It's one thing to read of them in the *Necronomicon*—but to actually find them here, as physical things—amazing!"

"I've never seen anything like that godless divinity," she told him, staring with eyes aghast at the beast above them. "You expect it to spread those wings and fly off any moment, it seems so lifelike."

"Did you ever read that tale by, I think, Dunsany—about the jade gods who were thought to have departed from their mountaintop thrones? He could have been writing about this magnificent devil, which looks ready to vacate this place in search of mayhem. How spectacular to confront a thing of whispered legend."

"I know that the world overflows with freaks—but *why* would anyone want to worship such a ghastly thing?"

"No, this is not a deity, Josephine. It's...a kind of soul symbol, mostly identified with a cannibalistic cult that is rumored to be but quasi-human. Freakish indeed. There's some who think this thing is a representation of the Hounds of Tindalos—but those fiends are 'hounds' in title merely. They're more like an amorphous black shadow or mist, similar to Shub-Niggurath. We can't really understand these things, since they filter from a dimension that has no semblance to terrestrial matter. They are utterly *other*." He smiled at her incomprehension. "I haven't explained a lot of this to you because I wanted you untarnished by lore and legend. My hope is that your mediumistic endowment can connect with the transcendent nature of the magick that was here evoked."

"I've explained to you that my abilities are merely instinctual. I've never had much interest in them until I saw their potential for bringing me money. I'm little more than a media sensation."

He squinted his eyes at her and curled his lips sardonically. "I know that's your line, your prosaic pose. But, no—you're far more than what you allow publically. You see, I *am* experienced with such things. Intimately so, if I may so phrase it. I recognized at once your authenticity when I attended your performance and blew your mind, although you hid your dumbfounded reaction well from the others in your audience. I knew you needed guidance, and I confessed I needed abetment. Thus, here we are."

"It was your money that seduced me, Matteo—not your mission. I had no real interest in traveling to this alien land and trudging to this godforsaken place."

"And yet you're captivated. You can taste the aura of the place, I can tell by the look in your eyes. Now I want you to help me evoke its alchemy so that I can name it in formula and become the sorcerer I

Some Unknown Gulf of Night

was meant to be. It's not enough to conjure smoke and wind and shadow—such picayune elementals. I want to elicit the slumbering necromancy that can educe something as tremendous as that atrocious monster. I want to raise fiends with whispered words of thaumaturgy, perform the miracles forbidden in the *Necronomicon,* to taste the occultism that blessed Abdul Alhazred with rich madness. I want to see beyond the pale auroras and faint suns into those other dimension and taste their secrets, as the beings represented by these pygmy idols did. Oh damn, it's beginning to snow again. We've little time."

Josephine sighed. "What would you have me do?"

"Commune with this rare realm."

She shivered at the thought, for such secret conference had already found initiation. Some remnant of the region's past had conjoined with her brain and blessed with vision. She moved before one of the stone idols, knelt deep in snow before it and pushed away the white stuff with which it was covered. Her gnomish companion gasped at what was then revealed, for the idol wore a mask of gold on which an emblem had been etched upon the brow. Josephine studied the totem's mask for some moments, and then she clutched it with gloved hands and pulled it free. The rough-hued face thus revealed was ghastly, ferocious, quasi-human—yet vaguely familiar. "It resembles you, Matteo."

He did not seem to hear her. "Put it on," he whispered. "Let it meld with mortal flesh."

"No," was her firm reply as she turned to lift the mask to him. "This was not meant for my kind. Only they of your ancestral blood may don the yellow mask. You were right to bring me here. I have communed with the prehistory of this realm—it plants pictures in my brain and sensation in my flow of blood. How odd, to taste a memory of carnage on my tongue. Strange aeons have now passed, and old hunger must be answered. Let us satisfy it now."

She brought the mask to her mouth and kissed it, and her companion saw the crimson beads with which her lips bequeathed ceremony. Again, she offered him the mask. He removed his gloves and took hold of it, and he shuddered at the sudden rush of ancestral memory. Turning to acknowledge the beast of black jade, Matteo pressed the mask against his face as the snow continued drifting from the sky. As he peered through eyeholes he imagined that the silver snow turned crimson. A stench of sacrificial slaughter choked his throat and made it difficult to breathe, to speak. No matter. She spoke for him, to the red wet air. He saw the thing that answered her, the smoke that rose from the jade devil, that sentient shadow-cloud with jaws stretched wide; the thing that, drifting to him, clouded vision.

She watched the mask fall from the place from which his face had been eaten away, but before his corpse collapsed she snatched the amulet from around his neck and slipped its cord around her own. Bending to her knees in gathering snow, she fondled the mask and lifted it above her head, allowing its glistening gore to rain upon her famished mouth.

XVI

We went, we three, to seek the secrets of the haunted place, to pierce its mystery. We had learned of it in a madwoman's dream diary, which she had kept while confined at Arkham Sanitarium. Sonia Orne was a poetess and biographer of unlucky versifiers, and we had been enthralled by her imaginative recollections of Justin Geoffrey and Edward Pickman Derby. She was of ancient Arkham heritage, her great ancestor none other than Jeremiah Orne, who imparted the books and funds that led to the establishment of Miskatonic University. It was Samuel among us who had been intensely drawn to her history, being a poet of peculiar cast himself; and it was he who had secured Miss Orne's private diary from the fellow who had stolen it from the madhouse wherein he had once been himself confined. The fellow was still slightly mad, and Samuel feared that this fellow might destroy the diary because of the bad dreams it seemed to instill within his prosaic skull. Samuel, having inherited a fortune from his wealthy Jewish sire, had easily procured the secret diary for an exchange of golden coins. There was no indication in Miss Orne's chronicle as to how she had discovered the existence of the forgotten burying ground, although there is mention in her journal about the dreams that caused her to don a dress of yellow silk and a death-head's mask and dance in a local cemetery where, exhausted, she would fall onto the ground and dine upon its dirt. (It was such behavior that convinced her relations to enshrine her at the asylum.) Strangely, the freak who sold Samuel the diary was also fond of dressing in a yellow frock and wearing a pallid mask, and it was he who suggested that he, too, knew the whereabouts of the secret mound and its sarcophagus that had been mentioned in Sonia Orne's diary. Indeed, after one sexual incident, this fellow lunatic had drawn a map indicating how to find the forgotten burying ground and its mound on which a spectral woman was said to dance by light of moon.

We journeyed to the edge of Arkham in Maurice's old jalopy, down a narrow road that became more and more treacherous, until we reached the place where the road had been split as if by some subterranean upheaval. Thus Moe parked his car and we packed our gear and walked until we reached the spectral hollow, entering into it as the heavens turned a curious shade of hazy blue-violet. We trekked until we found, at last, the lonesome place; we could feel

Some Unknown Gulf of Night

its incredible ancientness in our mortal bones. The mound was half-hidden by a thick growth of willows, but the fading light was enough to reveal the queer catacomb that had been built into it, the stone of which might once have been white but was nigh black with hoary age. Diseased black growths of grass and vines dangled over the edge of the roof and mingled with thick webs. Three stone steps three inches in height led to an iron gate, and it took all three of us to coax the thing to swing on its protesting hinges. The vault's cramped chamber was chillier than the air outside, and I lit my antique lantern so as to lighten darkness and thus investigate the single granite coffin that lacked lid or occupant. What was that draught of cool air that breathed upon my ankles? Hunkering beside the crypt, I found the crevice through which a chilly zephyr issued.

"Fellows," I spoke as I stood, "your assistance please." They gazed at me uncomprehendingly as I indicated the oblong cist and, leaning against it, began to push one end of it with sturdy hands. Still puzzled, my companions came to my aid and we struggled until the coffin began to slide over the floor's smooth stone; and Samuel let out a yell when he came close to tumbling into the pit that we exposed. I wrinkled my nostrils and coughed. "That is the effluvium of the very pit. No, Maurice, don't shine your modern flashlight's beam into the depths—for my antique lantern's glow is far more apropos in aiding our descent. Use caution as we traverse those cracked and narrow steps, they were not designed for feet like ours." I held my beacon high as the others slipped their torches into their packs, and I smiled as Samuel removed Sonia Orne's diary from a pocket and held it as if it were some treasured talisman. Entering the aperture and setting one unsteady hand against a cold and clammy wall, I began my descent into the labyrinth.

"I feel like we've entered one of your wild stories," Maurice told me, and he tried to laugh although the noise was not convincing.

"Or one of my dreams," I responded as I peered into the pit. It was unnerving, I confess, that the journey into the abyss took so long a time, took us so deeply down into the under-earth and seemed to warp time itself. The wretched airstream continued to hurl its foetor into our faces. When at last we did reach level ground I shouted at the cavernous space encountered and the litter of yellow bones therein. Numerous dimly-discernable archways led in a plethora of directions. "This is a dream indeed," I whispered, "a veritable phantasm."

I moved toward one earthy archway, stepping over bones as we traversed damp sod, earth that was at times so soft that I feared it would sift beneath our tread and open so as to drag us down to deeper nightmare. The draft of nefarious effluvium had somewhat dissipated, but its nastiness clung to our clothes and hair, so that we resembled an assembly of shuffling cadavers who followed a death-light to some obscure destination. And then we entered an-

Some Unknown Gulf of Night

other opened space, and we shouted in amazement at the sight before us—for it was nothing less than what remained of a decrepit building of disintegrating wood. The silence was absolute as I approached the narrow tilted plank that was all that remained of a door, and I spat disgust as the wood crumbled at my touch.

"You're not seriously going inside, Howard," Maurice protested. "The place will crumble on top of you, just like a House of Usher. The floor will split beneath your foot. Fah, I've never seen anything so dirty and diseased. It's a veritable carcass. What have we stumbled on, some forsaken town in which something so vile occurred that it was necessary to build new ground over it and hide it from sane sunlight? A place of buried transgression, a madness out of time?"

Samuel's voice sang to us. "It is a burial of time, where tomorrow will never come." Maurice cried as the young Hebrew pushed past me and entered the edifice. I did not hesitate to follow him into what appeared to be a kind of parlor where the few furnishings were crumbling grime-coated antiques such as I had never encountered. In the dim place beyond were three narrow hallways, into one of which my youthful friend had trod. Sighing, I advanced after him as he passed a number of rooms, each of which contained a bed. I was annoyed by the sound of Moe's rough laughter and his hand on my back.

"It's a bordello!"

"So it appears," I quietly concurred, watching as Samuel reached the end of the hallway and pushed open the final door. He vanished

W. H. Pugmire

into the adjoining room, from which a pale illumination gradually filtered. He had turned on his flashlight. Maurice rushed past me and entered the room, but I was hesitant; for I sensed that whatever the room held would be an eerie key to the mystery upon which we had been guided by the diary of a dead woman. But at last I gathered nerve and crept toward the room, where my fellows were shining their torches onto a small bed and its occupant. I surveyed the petite mummy that was attired in a tattered gown of yellow silk. A wig of deepest crimson covered its dome, and its eyelids were weighed shut with tarnished coins. I frowned at the soft sound of Samuel's lamentation, which I could not comprehend, and said nothing as he switched off his flashlight and floated to my side. Raising the Orne diary to my lantern's firelight, he turned its leaves until coming upon a poem that had been scribbled in faint script. He touched the page with caressing fingers as he recited.

"I amble to your dark and quiet room
And kneel before your bed of final rest.
I wear a splash of your preferred perfume
As in your yellow party frock I'm dressed.
I see my shadow pirouette and lift
My silhouetted arms to hidden skies.
Oh, take beloved's final precious gift—
I kiss the pennies pressed upon your eyes.
I clutch your glossy tresses with one hand
And move into the daemon danse you taught.
I listen for one final hushed command.

Some Unknown Gulf of Night

I twist your wig into a tighter knot.
I bend to press unholy lips to thine.
My last embrace will be your ever-shrine."

My lamplight caught movement as Maurice glided to a small table and picked up the quaint object found thereon, an antique music box composed of white gold. How loud it clicked as he wound it, and how impossible it seemed that the relic began to play a delicate melody. I watched as Samuel handed me the Orne diary and shuddered as he pressed his lips to mine for one sweet kiss. Moving from me, he reached for the dead thing's crimson wig and slipped the filthy thing over his hair. Lifting his graceful arms he moved in time to the sound of the music box. How queer his silhouette moved across the walls, and how the entire room trembled at his tread. The melody from the box subsided—yet there was music still, muted and distant. Samuel spun toward one wall, to where there should have been a window but was instead a rectangle sealed with solid stone. I quaked at the sight of it, for it suddenly reminded me of a nightmare that had recently disturbed my sleep, a vision of a house of death wherein a window was sealed with such a block of stone. And this evocation of unearthly melody became hauntingly familiar the more I listened to it, and I knew that it was a noise that would herald doom.

"No," I whispered as my fellows touched the sealed window and struggled so as to push the stone away. At last it moved and fell over the edge to the other side, and we all choked at the stench that wafted to us from the aperture. The noise was now distinct—the hideous piping that mocked the music box's enchanting tune. The space beyond the window's rim was illuminated with black-violet phosphorescence. We could just make out the alien tree that spread its writhing limbs, boughs on which seven buzzing spheres shimmered with unnatural radiance. Below the sentient branches of the unfamiliar dendroid stood a black figure, gaunt and lean and haughty, its outline fluctuating as if it were enshrouded in a robe composed of midnight. I could not make out any facial features except the octagonal eyes that shimmered as would golden coins. The uncanny composition commanded my attention and my eyes tried to focus on the shifting things that squatted on the ground before the eidolon and pressed cracked flutes to amorphous mouths. Now and then weird streams of diminutive lightning would spark among the seven spheres of the alien tree, flashes that revealed a vortex of nothing beyond the daemon and its tree, a hungry opacity.

"No," I wept as Samuel lifted himself into the window and crawled through its cavity, falling out of sight for one moment. When he rose the wig no longer covered his glossy hair. I watched him drift toward the daemon and stand trembling before it; and then he lowered to his knees as the creature offered Samuel its hand, which my friend began to lick. I shook into full wakefulness as Maurice began to move into the window-space. Turning, I fled from the room, out of the crumbling house, through the earthen labyrinth until I found the narrow steps that took

Some Unknown Gulf of Night

me into moonlight and fresh air.

My friends were never seen again. I miss them, and yet there are times when I seem to sense their presence, and the other ghosts with whom they keep company. I sink into an awareness of this especially when I dream, when Samuel's lithe silhouette spins before me and presses his phantom mouth to my cool lips. I feel the air chill over me as they bend above my sleeping frame of flesh, and I do not protest when they place their coins upon my eyes.

XVII

He heard the tinkling bell that sounded in a distant place and shivered in the cold, thin air. Thus he concentrated on sucking at his Egyptian cigarette and scowling at the scene spread below them. Perhaps, at another time and in a different mood, he would have been able to appreciate the appearance of the sky from the hill to which they had traversed, for the sky wore aspects of Whistler's fabulous *Nocturne of Black and Gold*, especially its clusters of yellow stars that spilled toward the valley beneath them and gathered as pools of golden ambiance.

"Are you coming in?" one friend inquired, standing near the entrance of the isolated hillside club.

He waved the human pack away with the hand that held his gold-tipped cigarette. "One moment. I wish to commune with this eastern sky. Perhaps I can coax the hidden moon to reveal herself. I adore the moon and her chilly kiss. Proceed without me, and I shall follow anon."

His party shrugged and turned away, and he watched them flow as gathered flesh through the

Some Unknown Gulf of Night

double doors of the hillside edifice. "*Au revoir*," he muttered, turning his eyes so that they could follow the zigzag line of the pitted wall of stone that looked, to him, like some petrified python that had fallen into a slumber from which it would not arouse. They had to pass through a portal in that massive wall so as to reach their destination, and he wondered why such a wall was required to separate the lonesome hillside from the region of the valley town in which his people were vacationing. Finally, exhaling one final cloud of tainted smoke, he crushed the remnant of his weed beneath his foot and turned to examine the building's double doors. What had his companions called the place—the Club of Seven Dreamers? The mundane building would never inspire his dreaming, what with its dull and weathered planks so poorly put together. How it tilted and sagged, and how hesitant he was to enter its confines.

The sound came to him again from some distant place—tinkling bells. Turning to investigate, he scanned the other regions of the hill and detected a figure far away, a being cowled like some dreary monk. Yet as he looked longer, he could not be certain that it was a fellow being at all, for now it resembled an irregular chimney on which a small silver sphere had been painted near its top. Then the image began to blur and sting his eyes, and thus he turned away and shivered once again in the thin air that caused such discomfort when breathed in; and so he approached the double doors and entered the silent club.

He was instantly deflated as he encountered the creature who awaited him, a nude nymph with gold and silver crystals sprinkled onto her pubic nest. Her petite breasts pointed their ruddy nipples to him and he smirked as, fingering one, he whispered, "You should have been a boy." Handing her his heavy coat and wooden cane, he walked past the tables at which figures bent together suggestively, but as he scanned the room for his party he was disappointed by their absence. Perhaps they had wandered into some adjacent chamber.

Something caught his attention, the suggestion of a sound, and as he turned to heed it he beheld a figure that transfixed him—a cloaked creature that stood before a wall of obsidian liquid. Beguiled by androgynous beauty glimpsed beneath the figure's hood, he approached the unmoving youth and marveled at its supple limbs, fine pale face, and tantalizing phallus. Moving his hand, he touched the metal bell worn on a piece of cord wound 'round the handsome neck, and he shivered at how soft the metal felt, as smooth as cool new death. Tightening his fingers to the bell, he shook it once and laughed at its tinkling reply; and then, shutting his dazzled eyes, he leaned toward the cowled head and touched mouth to mouth. The phantom's kiss sucked him into the lagoon of night that rippled as liquid wall, and when at last he had imbibed his fill of passion and pulled his face away, he discovered that they had spilled into a dusky chamber wherein seven coffin-shaped urns smoked upon their tripods. Approaching the nearest urn, he peered into its depths and beheld an obscure image that might have been a face composed of fog and shadow, in which yellow eyes ignited. He blinked as these combustive elementals rose in coils of incense and gathered in the dusky aether as a cluster of yellow stars; and as he watched his name was whispered, so that he turned to acknowledge the summons.

The androgynous beast filtered to him through the gathered smoke and shadow, and he could not comprehend its alternation; for the white epicene countenance had altered so as to appear more feminine, and its breasts had horribly expanded, and its golden phallus had sunk from sight. He stood, tilting freakishly, as the cluster of yellow stars blinked about the region of the creature's pubis, glistening in the moist and fragrant mound. Tilting more, he fell onto his knees before the being's sex and sucked in its sharp perfume.

As his nostrils expanded the yellow points that were daemonic eyes trembled with rising and whirled to him until they sank into his own eyes, which transformed as liquid orbs of altered jelly that saw through mundane dimension and beheld another plane.

A bell tinkled above him. Lifting his eyes to stare at the dead face beneath its hood, he saw the sphere that had once seemed a thing of flesh drift upward as a globe of lifeless lunar dust that cooled his dreaming face. He watched it hatch and spill its vision to him, and thus he understood.

XVIII

I climbed the ancient steps of the moss-thick tower and looked upon the terraced garden of dream, the place for which my weary soul had ached. I found the cavity of ruin in the tower's wall through which I squeezed my paltry flesh and bone, and then I leapt onto the high rough-hewn masonry on which I balanced for a while until intoxicated by the scent and sight below. Deliberately, I stepped into the air and shut my eyes, but I felt no impression of falling from the wall, felt nothing but the press of hands upon a rough-hewn place. Yet I knew that I had vacated the high and corrugated wall, and so I slowly opened my uneasy eyes and found myself bent over a stony walk within the garden of dream. Ah, the soft sunlight on my entranced eyes! Oh, what beauty in the lullaby of Nature all around! I rose and trod the rough-hewn path, stepping onto the smooth surface of an arching bridge and stopping momentarily to watch my golden reflection in the gentle water's course. I admired the handsome

Some Unknown Gulf of Night

structure of a white pagoda wherein a gigantic brass bell hung, and when I noticed the obsidian hammer resting upon a pillow of sculpted stone I decided that I would bang the implement against the bell before departing the entrancing place. I knelt beside the delicate boughs of a cherry tree and lifted handfuls of pink blossoms to the rose and yellow sky. My old dreams had not lied: the drowsy radiance of the place was enthralling, and the conjoined song of gentle river and whispered breeze lulled me toward an ecstasy of dream within a dream. Yet even as I closed my eyes I could still sense the yellow radiance of the sun upon my lids, an aura through which rose-hued shadows blossomed. Tears of joy trickled down my happy face.

I cannot recall the seduction of slumber, but suddenly I felt a chill upon my lips. I awakened in a terrarium of nightmare, my aching back against the trunk of a dead and fungous thing, my mouth against a barrier of glass. The still air was haunted by the echo of a mammal's wings. I staggered to my feet and tripped along a path of broken stone, past the gray and splintered pagoda where its tarnished brass bell had fallen and lay lopsided on the ground. I hobbled to the rough-hewn wooden bridge, and midway over its rotting surface I bent over so to glare aghast into the stagnant pool below. Sallow moonlight revealed my countenance of diseased yellow skin, a transparent sheath pulled tightly over the skull that held my desiccated brain. The wall was gone, replaced with an unending surface of glass coated with night's slime, an ichor that made climbing an impossibility. I wept until I heard the clanging of a cracked bell, and when I turned to peer at the damaged pagoda I beheld the eidolon that stood beside the tarnished bell, an implement in its hidden hand. Ah, perhaps I could use the black hammer so as to shatter the wall of glass! I flew to the phantom with rage and determination pounding my heart, but the creature did not fight me; rather, it handed me the mallet and seemed to study me, although I could detect no face beneath its cowl. I staggered to the wall of glass and smashed my tool against it, and so ferocious was my madness that the wall began to crack and split. I heard the cool air before it claimed me, the suction from Outside that plucked me through the splintered wall, into a nothingness that claimed me absolutely.

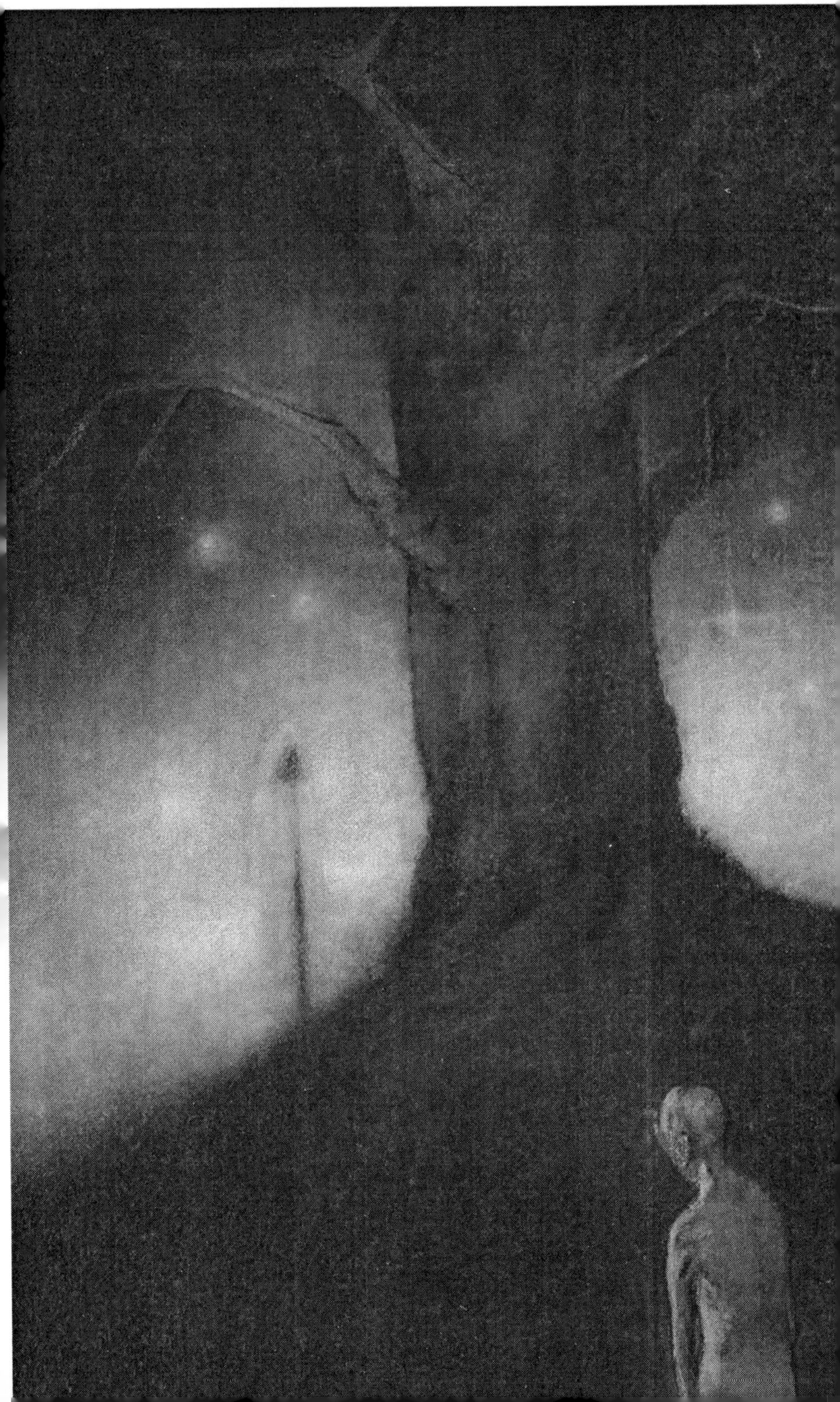

XIX

I hear the faint far ringing of a deep-toned bell as I carry you up the black mountain in this midnight wind. I have heard the call before, in deepest dreaming; but I do not imagine that I am dreaming now, this witching hour, for I feel too bitterly the sharpness of the clarion tempest; and I feel too sharply a pain in my ankles as I traverse toward the apex of the spectral peak with my burden in my arms. You seem to reassure me with your wide and frigid smile, and I bend to kiss your eyes in which I see reflected frosty starlight; and thus, although exhausted, I continue my trek beside the centuried wall that meanders the mountainous region. The pealing vibrations have ceased their sound, and now the thin and chilly midnight air is still and lonesome as, at last, we reach our journey's termination. Gently, I set your body onto the solid ground and lean, deeply breathing, against the antediluvian wall on which queer symbols, here and there, have been engraved; and I wonder at the sight of the occasional towers atop that unending length of masonry, and

Some Unknown Gulf of Night

cannot guess their function as, reaching toward the lunar sphere, they pierce the midnight air. And as I study one such thing, I imagine that a nameless fiend, winged and without face, glides to the conical point and, hanging there while grasping onto the tower's tip, makes motions to the moon with other paw.

    I frown at the slender archway that serves as aperture leading through the centuried wall into another place, and at the coaxing of the midnight wind I grasp your pale hands and pull you through the slit in stone, into another realm where wind and earth contain a deeper chill. I glance again at the tower on the wall, which casts its phallic silhouette on garden's ground, but do not see the imagined fiend without a face, and thus I turn to contemplate the holes with which the ground is pockmarked; and as I tilt beside the nearest burrow I smell a memory from deepest dreaming, and my mouth remembers strange remorseless appetite. I smile at you as one large hand claws the loose earth of the burrow and brings a handful of aromatic debris to my face; and I sigh as I wash the filth into my flesh as other hand lifts to the moon. I creep to you, my adoring wretch, and you do not complain as I touch you with my grimy hands and lift you so that your face, once more, is sheathed in ghastly lunar light; and, overwhelmed by your beauty, I bury my face within your hair as I trod the garden ground. Here is a weird white tree whose bark is as smooth as cadaverous skin, and so I set you beside its trunk and perform a dance in moonlight for your pleasure. Ah, your grin is wide; and I think that you would laugh if only you could recollect how to stretch your jaws.

W. H. Pugmire

I move merrily over an expanse of garden ground until, exhausted, I rest one hand against the centuried wall; and as I pant I see the huddled thing nearby, and when I approach this other inhabitant the moonlight reveals it to be a ruined thing of pulp and petrified bone, with a skull so cracked that one might imagine it to have been smashed against a wall of glass; and as I bend over its remains I am overwhelmed by the rancid aroma of its ruination. I study the marks that perforate the exposed bone, and I close my eyes so as to taste dregs of recollection. But then the midnight wind whispers at my ears and brings the scent of rank vegetation and your sweet fragrance. Returning to you, I fall before you and bless your mouth with lover's passion, and then I fold your arms about my neck and lift you once again as, suddenly, bleak rain slips onto us from stormy sky. But do not fret, beloved, for there in the distance is the silent pagoda composed of crimson posts and roof of jade. We need but cross this wooden bridge so as to reach its shelter; but let us pause for just one moment and peer into the squalid pool below us and marvel at our sodden shadow on its liquid surface. Ah, the rainfall increases and savages our dreaming visages, and so we rush into the shelter of the pagoda. This ivory pew, as lovely as the skin that sheathes your bones, will serve as couch until the storm has passed, and you look so lovely as I lay you onto it. Yes, I am intoxicated by the violence of the storm, and you smile at my clownish antic as I fling my limbs into the liquid air and dance on soggy sod. Then, returning to you, I notice the wooden mallet on its pillow of sculpted ebony, and with that mallet in my hand I

Some Unknown Gulf of Night

approach the massive bell of brass that hangs from its post within the pagoda. I touch the surface of the bell and examine the figures embossed thereon, those devils poised like furtive apes. I lift the hand that holds the mallet and wink at you, and then I bring it down.

Ah, the deep-toned reverberation! It seems to shake the earth into which its vibrations sink as summons. I pound the massive bell once more, and its heavy sound dispels the storm so that, once more, we see the daemon moon; and in that dead sphere's suggestive illumination I watch the shaggy shadows that ooze from out their earthy pits within the garden ground. I see them raise their canine snouts to Luna's influential light and move into a bestial kind of danse. They pour through pits and call to me, their cousin. Some climb the wall and mount the ancient spires so as to adore the moon with eyes of jade and paws that move symbolically. Some seep toward the remnant of flesh and bone that stains the dirt near one portion of the wall, and the stench of that mortal husk so clutches them that they raise their snouts so as to howl deliriously. And one last shape lopes toward us, my love, and grins rapaciously as it sniffs the aura of your decay; and then together, kindred creatures, it bends with me to kiss your chilly breasts.

XX

I walked along the wide surface of centuried wall and peered below me into the ghoul-haunted garden as the north wind's swell washed over my yellow robe and frolicked with my length of hair. My arms, outstretched, waved hands above the twisted trees on which enigmatic emblems had been chiseled, and I allowed my nails to trace similar insignia into one arm. Falling to bended knee, I reached into a pocket of my robe and touched the shard of charcoal that was therein; and then, taking out the shard, I pressed its porous substance onto the surface of the wall. The charcoal had been prepared from essence of strange vegetable and animal, and its alchemical properties when in my thaumaturgic hand were profound. I drew an emblem with the black substance, and then I stood and danced in rising wind upon my icon. Lifting arms to distant starlight, I made the Elder Sign to whatever may sense it within the haunted heavens; and although to make that sign with one's paltry digits of flesh and bone can be a

Some Unknown Gulf of Night

painful process, I was determined to sink into some hidden depths of nightmare's well and find one special place. I returned the shard to its pocket and peered into night's dark chasm, and saw the thing that fell through cosmic aether—the lean descending one that stretched bat-like wings as it circled to our little world; and as it fell each star touched by its tip of wing dimmed a little, or died entirely. I marveled as a sheen of ghastly moonlight played upon the horned creature's smooth black skin as it perched on one of the basalt towers of the antediluvian wall.

Standing on my insignia, I moved fingers to the moon, and I fancied that the beast observed me although it wore no countenance. Yet as I stared at the place where there might have been a face I suspected a suggestion of some sentient thing in its blankness; and as I peered more deeply into its nothingness my eyes grew heavy and my mind began to mist. Before my eyes were completely closed I saw the wings stretch again as the beast lifted from the tower, and I felt the air nearest me move in waves although I heard no sound. Slippery paws, cool and damp, wrapped around my neck and ankles as I was lifted off the wall, into thin air.

My jaws stretched wide so as to express with delighted howling my rapture as we voyaged beyond mundane time and space, beyond the wall of sleep, into an undimensioned region that was my intimate nightmare; and I felt the spectral atmosphere protest as one of flesh and blood presumed to invade the world that accepted naught but dreaming psyche. I was set beside the ruins of a castle that seemed familiar, and as I studied its charred remains a flock of smooth black things emerged from its cavities—the kindred of the night-gaunt that had stolen me from the earthly realm and brought me to my land of nightmare. They circled around and over me, and some drew near so as to weave prehensile talons into my hair and press their blank heads to my mortal mouth. They took hold of my black hands and led me into dance beneath the pallid moon, which looked far more ghastly in this place of incubus than in my other demesne. My mortal bones trembled ferociously as I danced, for they felt intently that they were not to exist within this realm of malign daemonic vision. We danced in silence, moving away from the ruined castle and down a path that led eventually into a necropolis in which there grew thick pale willow trees. Upon one dilapidated seventeenth-century slab of white marble, which had been partially engulfed by the trunk of a willow that grew next to it, sat a dark thing that sucked unwholesome nourishment from a relic that had been excavated from the hoary, charnel earth. The night-gaunt that had stolen me from the waking world went to the rubbery creature and extended one impossible paw, to which the ghoul bent so as to kiss what passed as palm; and then the gaunt arose and vanished into the midnight aether, followed by its brood.

"Richard," I called as I approached the white slab—for I had known this beast in intimate dream. He gazed at me queerly, as if it had been a length of time since any voice had so saluted him; or perhaps it was the sound of my waking voice that startled the surrounding air and splintered the creature's brain with recollection. Sitting beside him, I exhaled my witch's breath onto his mouth, until finally it moved.

"I have known your eidolon, but to have you here in flesh is unspeakable. You corrupt our realm with your blood and bone."

"Ah, sweet corruption," I cackled. "Be at peace. I have come to give you a relic of your mortal art, the gift that you have lost in ghoulishness. I know the ache that taunts what was once your mortal heart. Give me your hand."

He paused for but one moment, and then held out his hand, into which I placed the shard of charcoal that I had taken from its pocket. He gazed at it with uncomprehending eyes; and so I took it from his palm and moved its porous surface across one small section of the white slab on which we sat. I stood and placed the shard into his hand once more as he stared at the name of "Pickman" that I had written on the stone. His wide dark brow furrowed as he thought, and then thought transformed into recollection. Hesitantly, he pressed the charcoal onto the slab and began to work. When he was finished, we both admired the semblance of the face that he had worn in the waking world; for portraiture had always been his forte.

"When we met in dream," I whispered, "you led me to an archway through which I caught a glimpse of an audient void wherein one might encounter Crawling Chaos. Do you remember?"

"I have a faint recollection," the ghoul replied as he gazed at his sinister portrait.

"Show me the place again," I commanded.

The creature sighed, then shrugged. "'Tis but a little distance." He loped clumsily through the burying ground and I followed, past an ancient stone church with crumbling spire, until coming at last to a lonely mausoleum, which we entered through a grating of ornate iron. Descending some few steps, we moved into a vault of marble shelving on which there rested oblong boxes in various states of ruin. My companion lowered to his knees and began to work at one portion of the stone floor with his strong inhuman nails, until at last he pried open a portion of that floor that proved to be a slab covering an aperture. Violently, he hurled the heavy slab away so that it slid from us across the smooth floor, and then he leaned over the edge and gazed into the descending darkness as he wheezed from his exertion. Lifting his face to peer into my eyes he smiled, and I saw a semblance of the man he once had been within unwholesome features. Saying nothing, he climbed into the aperture and began to scale its wall. We climbed down a cylinder of rock, finding whatever holds we could for hand and foot. I could see still, if dimly, and laughed at the silent bats that flocked about us. The air became heavy and moist the more we climbed, and it took on such a strange aura that I felt as if we were descending into a dream within a dream. I sucked in its delicious decay as, at last, we reached a surface of damp stone floor, and I looked about the place that looked as if it could have been a castle's dusky chamber.

I watched the thing that had been Pickman glide stealthily through darkness, toward what I at first mistakenly thought to be an archway leading into a similar chamber; but then I saw the blurred semblance of his ghoulish form appear before him,

Some Unknown Gulf of Night

and knew that his hand, outstretched, touched a surface of black and polished glass.

XXI

I approached the standing mirror before which the denuded ghoul stood and admired its tarnished frame which had been maligned by hoary age, and when I stopped beside my familiar I noticed the rare and peculiar symbols that were embossed on the metallic border, glyphs that were emblems of occult things. Scrutinizing my muted image on the foggy glass, I disliked the refulgence of my yellow robe that clashed with the murkiness of the silent place wherein I stood, and so I pulled it from me and let it crumple to the floor. My inky skin looked most appropriate in my surroundings, matched as it was by the rubbery tissue of my ghoul companion. I stood behind him and snaked my arms around his neck. My body pressed against his cool inhuman hide, and I was disappointed that my action did not have the effect on him as it had upon those men who melted at my touch, nor did he shudder at the pressure of my teeth upon his neck. Thus I turned my attention to the icons embossed upon the mirror's

Some Unknown Gulf of Night

grimy frame, and my mouth was very near Richard's tapered ear as I pronounced the language of those secret signals—and it was my whispering that moved my beast to shudder. Sighing soft laughter, I ran my fingers to his loins as I sank to knees and kissed his buttocks. I drank in his rank foetor, that rich aroma. I turned him around and kissed his impotent sex and then clutched his flanks with my nails and tugged him to his knees. Our mouths met, and it was then that I tasted a remnant of the one thing that he desired—the decay of death with which his tongue was coated. My nail sliced his face, and his blood was so black that I could scarcely see it against his dark elastic flesh—but its redolence was overwhelming. With ecstatic tones I mouthed once more the formulae embossed upon the arch that held the dusky mirror, and as I gazed into that glass I saw the combined image of our nakedness ripple. And beyond our reflected silhouette another semblance blossomed, drifting toward us from some distant pocket of the void. It wavered like some crimson flare, an animation that flowed as fabrics red as sunset flame. He stepped gracefully through the tarnished arch and stood before us, silent and lean and cryptically proud, and the triple crown perched upon his dome was made of an identical metal as the mirror's frame and wore the selfsame icons.

The Black One offered his hand to my compatriot, who took and licked it. The Black One nodded his approval, and then he lifted a foot and ruthlessly kicked the ghoul away. He then considered me and said, "You have debauched the realm of dreamland with your mortal presence in this place."

"We witches are a clever brood," was my reply.

W. H. Pugmire

"We flow where we will."

"And yet you cannot reach your desired destination without my assistance."

I bowed my head in acknowledgement of his wisdom. Reaching out, he took hold of my hair and pulled me upward. He breathed onto my eyes, and I shivered at the diabolic vision that consumed my splintered brain. His hot hands wove into my hair and reached into my skull, and I felt him clutch my brain and hurl it forward, where it smashed through a surface of black mirror. The rank smell of blood cocooned me as my vision cleared, and I turned so as to peer dimly through the threshold, into the chamber from which I had been heaved, the room where my discarded carcass was sprawled upon the blood-soaked fabric of my yellow robe. I watched the ghoul that crept to my cadaver and began to feed, and then the image of that realm of dream evaporated.

A multitude of desert wind thronged about us and whispered of forgotten things. My soul was kissed by silver moonlight as we flitted across a field of sand toward a city of pillars. The strange Dark One who accompanied me lifted his hand to the moon, and I watched the curtain of blood that covered the disc and transformed the desert into a plain of gore; but then the desert sand siphoned the scarlet spillage as mad auroras of bright yellow and pale green rose beyond the rim. The Dark One moved his hand again, and the heaven turned mauve as the moon ignited into a disc of white inferno. We floated past the massive pillars on which I could espy the glyphs with which the tarnished frame of a black mirror had been embossed, and I could hear the enunciation of

Some Unknown Gulf of Night

those glyphs whispered on the daemon winds.

    We stopped before a titanic threshold of cosmic flame as Earth's dust was blown away by daemonic wind. The strange Dark One, behind me, howled insanely, and then his horrible mouth puckered and exhaled, and my final remnant of mortality was hurled as discarded debris beyond the flaming doorway.

XXII

The madwoman climbed the endless stairs that took her to the choking room that contained one single inhabitant, the notorious mystagogue of whom all Arkham had been whispering. They who had witnessed the disturbing exhibition spoke of it with fear clouding their uneasy eyes, and as she contemplated the troubled murmurings of the crowd, the madwoman heard a buzzing of recollection within her cracked skull—for she had once been a professor of esoteric poetry at Miskatonic University where she had dwelt on the fantastic poets such as Justin Geoffrey, Clark Ashton Smith and Edward Pickman Derby—seers who had also spoken of fantastic things. The intriguing rumors shared among Arkham folk were very similar to the themes evoked in the poetry of those bards, whose books she had managed to hold on to when madness had cost her the position at the college and forced her into a homeless existence, in which her nights were spent in a shelter beneath the steeple

Some Unknown Gulf of Night

of an ancient church. Curiosity had been pricked, and it was always charming to locate a new hovel in which to hide during daylight; and so she climbed endless stairs that took her to a little room in which a tall, gaunt woman of exotic beauty stood, a creature whose burnished hair of deepest red fell below her back. The eccentric wretch liked the warmth of the modest room, and she cherished its cozy silence, which served as contrast to the obnoxious world of men. She enjoyed looking at the enchanting woman whose gown of yellow silk clung seductively to a sensual figure, and she pondered the talisman that hung from its cord between the lady's full breasts—an amulet that depicted a faceless idol beside which two winged figures genuflected.

"Welcome," the woman spoke as she stood before a wall-sized screen on which dream-like images prophesied of mortal doom. "Please sit here, in this chair before me, and let us commune. You have appetite, I know. Look, on that table there—a tray of sustenance from which you will win a multitude of nourishment. Yes, set your thin book on the chair next to you and let me place this salver in your lap. Excellent." The lunatic marveled at the sight of the tray and its contents, for she had never seen anything like the seven iridescent apples of peculiar blush; and when she took one spherical object in hand and chomped into it, she was overwhelmed with awe at the taste that spilled into her mouth as the choked room darkened. She bit into the flesh again, as images began to move upon the walls, circulating pictures that coalesced into one single representation of an alien tree on which seven prismatic globes of fruit hung on writhing limbs before a backdrop of absolute obscurity. The quiet little room became haunted by a subtle song of windstorm that might have issued from far galaxies, a tempest that took on potency and attacked the tree, the substance of which deteriorated as scattered dust, although its seven spheres remained aloft in nothingness which they enhanced with sudden brilliance that burst from them as cosmic sparks. And then they too were caught within the cyclone, and spinning, they became a vortex of extraterrestrial tint, a spiraling pandemonium into which a madwoman might be sucked.

And so she was, drawn into a non-dimension that was awash with streams of violet illumination that glittered with the golden wreckage of seven dying suns. Yet she was not alone, for the magnificent black woman stood beside her as escort and took her melting hand as she transformed into a perishing bubble without form or place. Yet still some semblance of paltry human psyche remained extant, as mercury that spilled from black inhuman palm and leaked into another realm, wherein it frolicked before the features of daemonic camouflage that clothed Ultimate Chaos and danced to the playing of cracked flutes held in monstrous claw. Ah, glorious—the idiotic wail of that which transcends time, the fury without form or meaning, around which the transformed lunatic whirled as eternal advocate.

"That's a wondrous book." The sepulchral voice awakened the unfortunate one from dream's dimension.

"Yes, I used to teach it at University," the madwoman replied as she placed a protective hand over the book. She laughed scornfully as memory

Some Unknown Gulf of Night

emerged. "I had to pretend that it was symbolic—but my dreams had informed me otherwise, as only they can. The poet Derby was in fact a furtive campaigner of dark and secret things unknown to the plebeians who savored his lyrical aptitude alone, which they heightened because of his youth. Potent visionaries, the young. His art was a seductive force, as you are; and to sing his lines is to enter into an intimate relationship with sorcery."

She took up the volume, kissed it and pressed it to her bosom, from which her heartbeat sounded as a delicate throbbing in the gloom. She opened the book and peered at what she could make of the yellowed page; but she did not need to see the lines, for they dwelt inside her unhinged mind. However, before she could begin to recite, her hostess uttered song.

"I see the impish flock that moves in danse
About the Nameless Eikon so adored.
Their outlines play upon a ruined manse
As ghastly silhouettes of daemon-horde.
Oh, devil-horde that spread membranous wings,
That seeped from out the manse of ill-repute
And flock as nightmare's brood, obscene hatchlings
That move in an expression of tribute
About the Nameless Eikon of smooth stone,
Their embassy of Chaos absolute,
A monster mundane time cannot disown,
A deity dull man dare not refute."

The madwoman lifted her eyes in astonishment as the other sang the syllables of printed poetry; and then she shut her eyes and spoke the final couplet:

"And I, once dead-yet-dreaming, now awake

W. H. Pugmire

And reach into rich bedlam, and partake."

The black one smiled and removed the tray from the madwoman's lap. "What are you named?"

"I am Geraldine Worthington."

"Ah, Geraldine—look here, an ornamental hashish pipe from mystical Egypt. Now, let me ignite it with this length of match. Let me suck. Isn't that a sweet aroma? No, don't rise. Take this in your pretty mouth and let it transport you to a realm of delicious delirium and language. Heed not the sparks that flit between those incandescent suns, ignore the cosmic storm that weaves into your hair. Suck upon that stem and feel the coils of alchemy that curl into your skull, and then suck these lips I offer thee and taste of untold things."

Miss Worthington took the pipe and placed it in her mouth, drawing on the wooden stem so that airy nectar seeped into her mouth as cloud that floated to and claimed her brain, which hatched with vision. Smiling idiotically, she pressed her mouth to the other's and drank the elixir that was siphoned through her lips—that intoxicating lava. The seven suns turned above her head and sank into her eyes, with which she found new revelation. Her mortal essence moved through antediluvian forest until, at last, she stood before an obsidian obelisk that tilted over the obscene rubbery fiends that pranced around it. Some distance behind the black pylon stood a ruined manse through which a chill wind played through cracks and fissures, wailing as freakish intonation to which the dog-things danced. The madwoman ached to ape the dancing of the brood, one of which held horrid nourishment to its mouth; and she felt a tinge of unfathomable exhilaration as

Some Unknown Gulf of Night

the ghouls raised obscene paws to the enormous moon whereon shifting clouds formed one-thousand faces. She watched the terrible beams of that lifeless sphere of lunar dust fall onto the inhuman physiognomies, which it seemed to bleach and blur with reconstruction; and when those reformed visages turned to her the madwoman recognized them as the poets with whom she had been intellectually intimate. Wafting to them through shimmering aether, she took hold of hands and joined in their danse, shouting with them to the forlorn moon. At last exhausted, they ceased their movement, and she turned to the Frenchman's severe face, the stormy eyes of which she kissed. Noticing the bit of infant's brain that blemished the perfection of his mouth, she plucked it from him and held it to soft light. The poet smiled as he took it from her grasp and placed it below his nostrils, and he closed his eyes as he drank its sweet bouquet; and then, smiling, he moved it to the woman's mouth and placed it on her tongue.

The mystagogue stood before the obelisk and raised her countenance to moonlight, and the lunatic marveled as she watched the black face melt into one million more until, at last, it utterly diminished. Raising one majestic midnight hand, the strange Dark One caught residue of lightning that sparked between seven bursting spheres and aimed the voltage to the obelisk, the bulk of which began to split. Bat-winged brutes oozed from the cleft in stone and flowed aimlessly about the ruined mansion as other fiends, formless and fearful, took shape in mid-air and drifted to the black enchantress, before whom they genuflected as they raised cracked flutes to formless mouths. The coruscation emitted from the shimmering spheres melded with the melting black stone and reshaped it as the idiotic Lord of Chaos to whom the bat-fiends flew in adoration.

Stepping to the Faceless One, that triumphant avatar of ultimate pandemonium, the madwoman bowed so as to join the nebulous creatures in their adoration as their piping pierced the universe; and bending low she pressed her mouth to dark daemonic foot—the foot that, rising, contemptuously struck her mortal head.

XXII

My sense of wonder palpitates as I stand before the house wherein you lived when you penned your sonnet cycle, those poesy-dreams of alien fungi. Perhaps you were lured into the writing of your poems by Klarkash-Ton's sublime verse—for who could resist such influence? Or perhaps it was Melmoth's midnight apparitions that worked as aesthetic enticement. I stood before your home, wherein you dreamed of Dunwich and of Yuggoth, and I placed my hand upon the 10 with which the house was numbered—and I was overwhelmed with such potent emotion, such elevated sublimity, that I have not yet come down from ecstasy. It overwhelms me now, as I work on this sequence with which I pay honor to you, my Ever-Muse.

At times it seems impossible that you actually existed, so has my life been affected by the wondrous things you wrote. You seem mythic and remote, a Muse that visits only in my memory. The world in which you lived has drifted

W. H. Pugmire

down Time's unending stream, and as I try to visualize it in the violet-misted sky I see nothing but my own paltry era. The shimmering sun is a spectral disc within mauve heaven, a beacon that I follow down the rutted road that takes me to the isolated church, ancient and white-steepled, from which chimes no longer sound at death of day. I follow the slates until I find your name, which I whisper as I fall to bended knee. My bones shudder within their husk of wearied flesh as tears blur your name that is etched on weathered stone—the name to which I pay homage with my art. When they sank you into your futile depth of earth, you felt a failure in all things and sensed you would be forgotten for all time; but the Old Ones you awakened with your pen have never slept, and (dead-yet-dreaming) haunt the world anew, generation after generation. I seem to see one now, a blot within the violet-misted sky, an eidolon of chaos crowned by whorls of dead stars that it siphons from the universe; and as I gaze its strange dark hand catches a cluster of those cosmic embers and plants them deep within my mortal eyes. Thus aided, I behold strange towers and curious rivers as I dance through labyrinths of wonder beneath some vault of dream. And seeing this I ache to hold my pen and join you in eldritch song of Literature, to weave the words that express my sense of wonder. And from some pocket of this dream I feel the kiss of phantom wind that carries the evening chimes that reverberate from some ancient and white-steepled edifice in a land both alien and intimate, wherein

Some Unknown Gulf of Night

I can see the mystic mirage that is conjured by
the perfection of your supernal art.

XXIV

You called the individual names of the harpies that followed you through the streets of clay between tall and vacant buildings inhabited by regretful shadows. You relished the daemon-wind that whined betwixt the shards of shattered windows and matched the unholy litany of your antique violin with which you seduced the vixen at your heels. Ah, they followed you to the black canal and drank in the rich decay of its stagnant oily current, the sludge that oozed like black blood in some monstrous vein. Your hags, some of which had lost their tattered wings, crept near you on their silver-sandalled feet, their gnarled hands raised gracelessly to the daemon-wind, an element of which they caught and swallowed in their awful mouths. You led them past the tall and vacant buildings to the arch of displaced stone that spanned the black canal and then you stopped midway in crossing it so that they circled you with jerking limbs and moaned an accompaniment to your violin's wretched tune. Stupidly,

Some Unknown Gulf of Night

your vultures lifted legs that pirouetted in the idiot wind and moved to the edge of the arch of displaced stone, on which they balanced for one moment before falling over and into the stagnant slime. You laughed at their swampy song and continued to perform your heartless intonation as the daemon wind rose with what was left of your clumsy harpies: their yellow masks. You watched that cluster of false faces whirl from you toward the tall deserted buildings that rose like time-lost haunts of clay, and as you watched and grinned another element of wind bubbled upward from the thick canal. It claimed you as it caught your violin and snatched it from your hands; and as you reached impotently for your tool its strings were played upon by the daemon-wind, and at the squeal of that lullaby you moved your feet with following, coaxed once again into the city, above which arose a yellow mask of fog that spoke your miserable name.

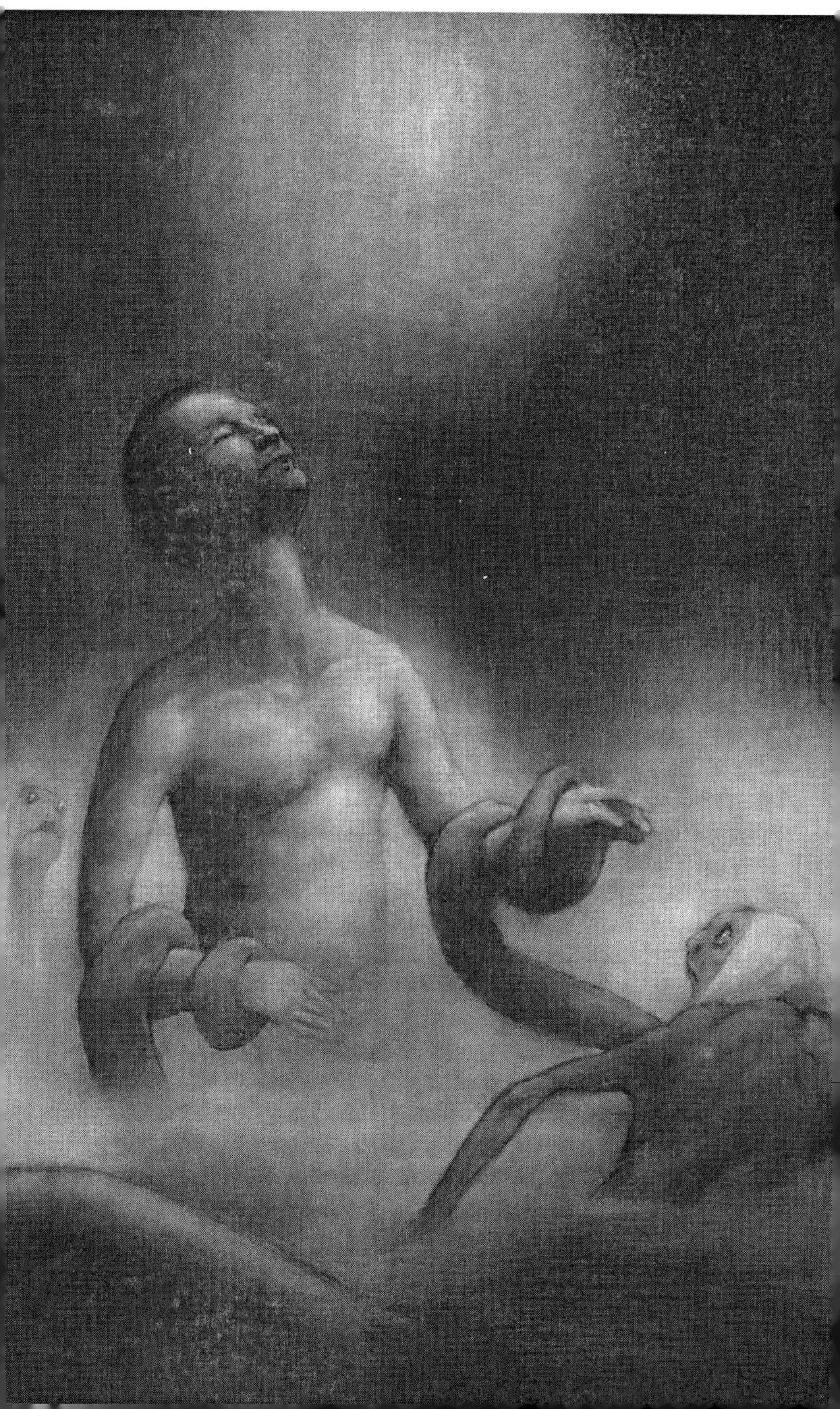

XXV

I awoke to daemon howling, and to the rattling of a tattered blind that flitted like some great bird's broken wing at the shattered window. I was not sad to see the pane's destruction, for I remembered witnessing an image on it that disenchanted me. I pushed myself with hands that pressed on shattered glass and rose erect. I combed my length of hair with fingers so as to rid it of splintered glass and other sullage. The thin air of the tall and vacant building that I inhabited had suffocated my dreams, and thus I vacated the choked room and climbed cautiously down the rough stone steps that took me from the urban tower, into untenanted lanes. An expanse of low and filthy cloud resembling a rippling yellow mask so unnerved me that I fled out of the dead city toward the stagnant canal just beyond the limits, the length of which I followed in my attempt to escape the infested metropolis and its pallid mask of cloud. I did not drop until the cityscape was a distant blur, and then I fell to knees on one cement ledge above the length of canal water. My eyes followed the serpentine flow until I saw the distant bridge that crossed over it, to a shelter of woodland. Something in the darkness of the woods beguiled my imagination, and thus evoked my daydreams summoned me to crawl beneath the mauve sky to what remained of an antique basalt bridge, over which I crept as the water beneath me coaxed with weird whistling. I had never known water to coo in such a way, and so I paused at the other end of the bridge and listened, until I learned the whistled tune, which I tried to imitate by pressing my cracked lips together. The second sound ceased at the infiltration of my descent and was replaced by a slithering that approached from underneath the bridge, from the hidden spot from which the structure's troll emerged—the hairless hermaphrodite who held a thin black reed in one bleached hand. I was about to bend so as to sniff the rank aroma of the creature's double sex when, from some deep place within the woodland, there came a low metallic sound that summoned me.

"Be wary of that false chime," my hobgoblin playfully counseled, but I refused to heed its coy admonition and, rising to my slippered feet, padded along the path into the labyrinths of woodland, past thick dark trees and gigantic boulders on which moss and fungi flourished. I could see, when lifting my eyes to the tops of trees, that the mauve sky had deepened into indigo, and I fancied that I could hear again, above those trees, the muted wailing of a banshee wind. The way sloped downward and led into a glade through which a river of blue and silver water frolicked, although it made no sound. But I

Some Unknown Gulf of Night

could not watch that water because I was entranced by that which stood above the wall of rock on the river's other side; and as I gawked a peal swept toward me from the black spire that tilted over an edifice of stones. I paid no heed to the voice behind me that murmured, "Beware, the false chime!" I climbed the hill of grassy patches and slate that led to the rotting wooden bridge that spanned the river and its rocks, and I tripped across the splintered wood and followed a narrow path until I touched the tabernacle. The high hills behind it were lush with silent growth that rose to the darkening welkin in which dim starlight began to wink. Bending to one square of deftly placed stone, I touched my mouth to the rough surface and shivered as its chilliness sank into me; and then I pushed away from wall and approached the entrance, where brass doors, hoary and unhinged, had fallen to the ground. I crossed the threshold and was instantly encased by an antediluvian aeration that christened my physiognomy with subtle moisture. Shadowed by my epicene mutant, I propelled through thick gloom and passed into an uninhabited chancel. The outside light had extinguished and thus I could not see my way too clearly, and so I reached for guidance to the wormy pews that smelled of perished prayers. I approached the silhouette of an altar as a sudden effulgence of moonlight beamed through the stained glass window high before me; yet as I studied that window I could not comprehend its image, which might have meant to convey some unrepentant creature pent in hell. And yet—something in the form of that black figure composed of dusky glass seemed familiar, and I tried to study it until a cloud obscured the lunar light and the window's image became a nebulous afterthought.

I heard once more the moan of daemonic wind from outside the edifice, and as I peered into obscure corners I finally noticed the second threshold, narrow and obscure. Wandering to it I discovered a circular stairway of rough-hewn stone that rose to the hidden place above. As I began to climb I heard again, more loudly than before, the pealing of some great bell. I paused to hear another warning from the freak that followed me, but instead there came the eerie piping of a flute. Ignoring the noise, I climbed until I reached the third threshold that led me into the belfry. The choked compartment was closed by three walls on which were fitted arched and unstained windows of impressive size. I could smell the grey thing that leaned against one enormous bell that was savaged by a crack in its metal. The amorphous shape sniffed the air and pushed away from the bell, and as it flowed to me I fancied that it was a breathing eidolon of the image I had detected on the stained glass window above the altar. Pressing its significant nostrils to my shroud, it drank deeply of my decay; and then it spun me around and thrust me toward one arched window, upon which was reflected my remains. I moaned as black memory awakened and the chamber echoed with the ghastly piping of some flute that was accompanied by the mocking wind outside the tower. I shuddered as my husband wrapped his rubbery arms around me and buried his wide mouth into my hair.

XXVI

None in our artistic circle had seen or heard from John in the nine months since his return from Prague, and although we had grown accustomed to his reclusive ways we had begun to wonder. John had inherited the old Whateley place on a hillside about one mile from town, a residence that aided his hermitage. Through laziness or indifference he had allowed the place to run down, not seeming to mind the dilapidation; for he existed primarily in his imagination, the way some artists do, and neglected the outside world entirely when he could. However, he and I were friends, and he had promised that upon returning to the States he would begin work on a new piece for my museum of decadent art. I had grown anxious to finally see what, if anything, he had come up with, and so late one stormy afternoon I drove up the hill to his silent house and pounded on its door. I stood there for a little while as the wind washed a fine drizzle onto my face, but eventually I heard movement and saw a shadow form behind the door's window. It opened and he stood before me, and I could tell from the fevered light that shimmered in his dark eyes that he had been at work on some great thing.

"Gerald," he breathed, stepping aside and allowing me entrance into his demesne. "I've been meaning to call you. I've been laboring on the new project and I'm fairly satisfied with what I've managed to do." The calm tone of his voice did not fool me, I knew when he was in the throes of artistic ecstasy. But I said nothing as he took my jacket and placed it on a peg. "I did write you from Josefov, didn't I?"

"Yes, where you drank a toast to Kafka for me. Your card—I suppose you were too preoccupied to write an actual letter—mentioned something that you had found, some interesting item. That was the last I've heard from you in this length of time."

"Yes, I had found something inside a hidden alley shop. You know I have a talent for finding the lost and obscure haunts where one may stumble across some fabulous thing."

"The kind of shop where you find your extraordinary books."

"Exactly. That's always been a handy ancestral attribute, but I possess it to a keen degree. But, come, let's go up." Thus we climbed the stairs to the second landing, from where I could detect the spicy fragrance of scented candles from the attic rooms above—John refused to work at art in electric light. I always cherished my hours in the attic rooms where the ceiling was so low that it almost touched my dome, for it was a realm in which I felt absolutely at home—a world of grotesque art, where beauty and terror dwelt in happy cohabitation. Portions of the wall contained built-in shelving on which hundreds of books were packed, and there were other tomes that rose as twisted columns from the floor. A small bed with rumpled covers testified that John had been existing in the attic, as was his habit when possessed by creativity. I peeked through the arched opening that led into a second chamber and saw the easel on which a large painting had been covered with an expanse of yellow silk. Always unable to contain my curiosity, I stalked through wavering light, past the threshold and into that other space.

"Is this your new thing, John?"

"It's recent—but, no, that's not what I'm working on." I clipped fingers to the silk and lifted it from the canvas, and then I whistled. "Interesting, isn't it? Ring-around-the-roses is one of childhood's oldest games, internationally so. You know the commonly held notion that it represents the Great Plague of London in 1665, with the children aping death when they 'all fall down'—but that idea is now widely disputed. The so-called 'symptoms' described in the popular versions of the song don't fit well with the actual agonies of plague. You'll notice that I've made the faces of the innocents rather grim and mature, although I've tried not to make them overtly malignant. Still, their effect is unnerving, I hope."

"Yes, it's superb. But the attention is riveted to the desiccated figure around which the infants play, especially the uninviting face. You've captured in its stiff expression a kind of pure ecstasy, which is the direct opposite of the face of the one child who looks out at the painting's viewers. Most disturbing. One hardly notices the other subtle touch—those two blurs in the background that take on form the more one notices them and begin to suggest contemplative griffins with wings folded on their humped backs. Whatever do they represent?"

The artist shrugged. "Haven't a clue. They're the one aspect I imagined on my own. You see, this oil is a modification of another—work." He hesitated for some few moments, and then he ventured into one dark corner and removed a rectangle from its wall. Returning to me, he handed over the large and heavy-framed image, and I held its plate of glass to candlelight so as to study the yellowed photograph beneath. "That's what I wrote to you about from Prague, after finding it at a small shop in the Jewish Quarter. It's obviously quite old, yet its faded image commands attention. At first I thought it must be an etching that had been cleverly designed to mimic early photography, but now I think it's an actual print."

"It reeks of paganism."

"Doesn't it? Deliciously so. The figure looks like a thing carved from smooth pale wood, except for the skull, which looks real enough. But, god, what expertise it took to make that sculpture so resemble an actual corpse! The technique astounds me. Of course, the wee creatures haven't joined hands as in my painted representation; rather, they seem engaged in some form of maypole dancing, with each paw clutching a twisted strand of silken hair. At first I mistook the gnomes for naked children, but one can't when seeing the imp that has turned to glare into the camera's lens. I've never seen such savagery in a face. Those twisted features—ugh! It looks an embodiment of purest evil."

"Yes—it's vile. I must hang it in my forthcoming

exhibition. You'll loan it to me, of course."

"Erm—no. I have something else in mind for you." He grinned at my little pout, took the photograph and set it onto a table. Then he took up a candlestick and crossed to the attic window, which he cracked open. "The tempest has passed, and the wind is pushing the clouds away from the new moon. Ah, the air smells magical after a storm. Let's go out back and I'll show you what I've been working on." So saying he held the candle aloft and followed its guiding light to the steps that took us down to the second landing, where the bright lights offended my eyes. I followed John down the stairs and through a hallway that took us to the kitchen, and then we exited through a back door into a spacious yard, a place I loved because of its relics. Here was the rusted antique automobile that had belonged to John's grandfather. There was the crude homemade guillotine that a suicidal cousin had constructed in his successful search for extinction. I followed John toward what looked like a canopy that he had erected at a place where grass did not deign to grow, and I heard him laugh softly as a rush of wind extinguished his candle's flame. Entering beneath the tarp that was the structure's roof, my friend stood beside a figure that had been draped with a covering of heavy fabric. "Help me with this, will you?" he asked as he dropped the candle to the dirt and took hold of one section of the fabric. Together, we lifted the covering from the statue beneath it, and I shouted a little at what was there revealed. The artist laughed again as he stood and admired his creation. "I knew that I didn't have the skill to duplicate the smoothness of that pale wood in the photograph, so I used bleached calfskin. Calfskin's perfect because it assimilates skin, and as you know I like to have my sculptures touched as a part of the spectator's experience of art. Go on, feel it. Sensual, in a ghastly sort of way. Isn't the wig fabulous? I had it made by Keziah, whom you'll no doubt recollect."

"What, that wretched transvestite performer we encountered in Arkham?"

"Just so. She's a marvelous wig-maker and I paid her a fortune for this. It's human hair, of course. It needs to feel authentic, not synthetic. It reaches almost to the ground, just like the hair on the thing in the photograph would were it not clutched by those goblins."

"And where are *your* imps?"

He hesitated. "I've—yet to construct them. Actually, I can't decide how they should look, what would seem more decadent. Those freaks in the photograph are certainly grotesque, but I rather like what I've done with my painting, those gnomes with childlike faces. I'm just about to start work on a second canvas to see what else I can come up with before I begin to build the rest of this piece."

He smoothed a hand over one artificial arm as I leaned nearer to examine the sculpture's skull, which looked odd in the lack of light. Bending low, I retrieved the candle and flicked my lighter to its wick. Bringing the flame near to the death's-head, I examined its surface with my fingers. "What the hell—is this a mosaic of, what, bits of bone?"

"Of course it is. The entire object had to be a construction of art. It took me a while to figure out where to find a deposit of bone fragments, but then I remembered when we drove through Dunwich and

Some Unknown Gulf of Night

you stopped so that we could climb that domed hill where that weird altar site was littered with fossils."

"You're saying that this skull is composed of bone fragments from Sentinel Hill? That explains its discoloration in places."

"Yes, some of the fragments were oddly charred or melted. Combined with others they form a nice yet subtle chiaroscuro."

A patch of cloud obscured moonlight, and I was glad to have the candle's feeble glow. Glancing at my friend, I noticed his playful expression in the eerie light. Reaching out, he clutched a rope of silky human hair. Smiling, I did likewise, and then I followed him as we circled the statue, dancing in the darkness to which we chanted.

Three weeks later, John's body was found in the backyard. Death had come as a small dagger that had been plunged into an eye socket. An acquaintance from the police force interviewed me and told me more details than perhaps he should have. The only fingerprints on the weapon were John's own. I was shown a photograph of the dagger but didn't recognize it as belonging to John's collection of occult ritual paraphernalia. John and I, one drunken evening, had decided to arrange to be each other's beneficiaries in case of death, but I was startled to discover he had made good on the joke. Thus I inherited his habitat and its contents, and I spent that first week after his death sleeping on the cot in his attic. My exhibition was now to be a memorial to my friend and his artistic genius. I had taken the eerie yellowed photograph and hung it on the wall above the bed—gawd, what a delirious affect that had on my dreams! Going through his things in the attic rooms I was slightly disconcerted to discover a folio of sketches that were studies of the evil gnome in the photograph; and yet I understand how such an image could engross a macabre artist, for the beast was like nothing one had ever experienced. Studying the sketches made me remember John's statue, which I hadn't looked upon because of its close proximity to his place of demise. Now I ached to be near it, to touch my fingers to the silky hide and woven hair. So I stalked down the steps, out of the house, into night.

The high moon cast its silver glow on the ground but could not penetrate the canvas that was the canopy's roof, and so I savagely uprooted the poles that held the structure up and let the lunar beams bathe the phantasm of flesh and bone and hair. Pressing my mouth to the thing's solid grin, I exhaled hot mortal breath into the cavity of bone, and then my hands clutched lengths of woven hair as I danced idiotically around the statue, my eyes awash with moonlight. I whistled at the two puffs of curious black cloud that drifted near the moon, and then I dropped to my knees and wept. My hands, pressed upon the dirt, found the curious indentations in the ground, prints that might have been the footfalls of malformed children that encircled the statue. My mouth made love to a leather foot that was effectively secured to the platform that kept the figure erect, and as I reclined I wrapped my arms around the creature's ankles and succumbed to dreaming.

Awakened by soft movement, I opened encrusted eyes and peered into the gulf of night. The moon was farther from me, and the black clouds had es-

Some Unknown Gulf of Night

caped the sky. I could see the prancing shadows in the corners of my eyes but could not yet directly acknowledge them. Instead, I shut my eyes again and pushed up onto my knees. Blindly, I sought one leather hand, and bending to it I kissed its palm. When again I opened my eyes I saw the distant place to which the two dark clouds had drifted, where they had settled so as to stretch their great black wings. The gnomes circled me in danse, and I shuddered to see the naked malefaction of their wretched faces. The one I recognized from the yellowed photograph held a small dagger in his malformed mouth, and I did not dare to move when at last he approached and touched his mouth to mine. Thus was the exchanged completed. They stood dead still in the awful lunar light and waited. I lifted my eyes for one final glance at the mosaic death's-head, which bent so as to smile down on me. And then I removed the dagger from my mouth and lifted it to my eye.

XXVI

The artist, deaf and mute, had been my childhood friend, and it was he who taught me how to sign; and it was from him that I found the inspiration to become a poet, an artist of language as he was an artist of imagery. We had remained close up until the time of my unhappy marriage, and after my divorce I visited him infrequently. I had been so emotionally drained and defiled from personal torment that I became extremely reclusive, remaining alone after returning home each work day from my secretarial duties. When, at last, I began to work on a new collection of verse, I experienced a longing for artistic companionship, and so I made my way to Philip's small house and pushed the doorbell. The live-in housekeeper/cook answered my summons and led me to the wide ladder stepway that took one to the upper attic rooms where my friend did most of his work. I found him sitting before a canvas in bright electric light, and that puzzled me as it had always been Philip's habit to paint in candle-

Some Unknown Gulf of Night

light. We signed our greetings as I pulled a chair next to his and took his hands in mine, and then I studied the painting on which he was employed. It was a night scene, but one so exceptional that I was instantly captivated. The main image was that of a titanic three-sided lighthouse erected on an expanse of large flat rocks that spread as far as eye could see. No body of water was in sight. A full moon shot one solid beam of light to the top of the tower that contained the lantern room, although the lighthouse itself was entirely dark. What struck me so powerfully about the work was the combination of effects that Philip had evoked. The plane of large flat stones, the moon and the myriad pinpoints of stars looked entirely realistic; but the structure itself contained a quality of otherworldliness that perplexed me. It was like some fabled construction of biblical myth that had usurped a location in historic fact.

Philip turned to study my reaction to his work. "It's strange and effective," I told him as he watched my mouth. "Wherever did you come up with the conception?"

How odd, his timid smile. "I saw it in a dream," he signed as I held his hands; and as I clasped him I thought I detected a slight trembling of those hands, as if he had been moved by queer emotion. And then the especially weird occurrence took place. I heard a most peculiar sound outside the small attic window. How can I describe it? It began as a high-pitched ringing sensation deep inside my skull that grew in depth of sound and transitioned itself to some place within the gulf of night outside the window. It then deepened into a kind of low moan not unlike wind, or whispering, and within its sound one could almost detect an idiotic alien summons. Something in the unfathomable sound of it stabbed like splinters in my skull, and I cried out in dismay. I turned to Philip, to see if he had detected my alarm, although he obviously would not have heard my cry; and I grew cold with a kind of fear when I saw that he was staring at the attic window with an odd expression on his face, an aspect of *listening*. Rising, I released his tight hands and walked to the small attic window, which I opened. Cool air brushed my face as I stared into dark heaven, and at first I could not understand what I imagined was before me, a void of illimitable blackness that contained a kind of undulation, as if I stared at waves of liquid sea that moved from me toward cosmic nothingness. Sensing Philip at my side, I turned to gawk at him, and although his face was at first extremely serious, he slowly forced a smile and leaned so as to kiss my face. Then he turned to peer out of the attic window, and when I followed his gaze I saw that there was a moon and myriad stars.

That was the last time I saw my friend. The occurrence of his mysterious disappearance caused much talk in our circle of bohemia, especially when it was learned that he had left a list of instructions in which I was bequeathed his final painting. That these instructions had been legally arranged suggested that he knew he would be disappearing, and many expected to find his body in some lake or isolated location—but his escape from the world was absolute and he was never found. I arrived at his home, which had been left to his faithful companion, and she presented me with the large canvas, which had been wrapped with sturdy paper and twine. I

Some Unknown Gulf of Night

was surprised, upon returning home and removing that which covered it, to find that what I had was either an alternative painting of the same scene or a reworking of the original canvas. It was identical in many ways, except for the moon, which was now a decayed grey globe; and the lighthouse was no longer dark but illuminated with a kind of black-violet light that oozed from the lens of the lantern room into space, toward the dead lunar sphere. All starlight had extinguished. As I studied the image I was overwhelmed with a feeling of intense loneliness, and with a futility toward all aspects of reality. It was a depressing work, and it made my brain cold with a kind of horror for mortal existence. I was overwhelmed with a longing for escape, for some way to vanish as completely as Philip had.

I hung the painting, that night, over my bedpost. It had snowed that day and my apartment was chilly. It is my habit to sleep in the nude; I liked the feel of flesh against flesh, my legs wrapped around one other, my hands at breast or thigh. I went to my closet and found the heavy eiderdown that I kept there for chilly winter nights, and thus I was fairly comfortable when at last I retired.

But it was a sharp chilliness that awakened me, and I could not understand why no blankets covered me. I felt cold terror when, gazing upward, I did not see bedroom ceiling but rather an expanse of midnight sky in which a cold moon gleamed. I pushed myself to a sitting position on the large sheet of rock on which I had reclined and shivered in the wintry wind that assaulted my nakedness. The triangular tower of stone tilted above me, and out of its pharos there shone a blurred beam of dark radiance. Rising, I walked along the rocks to the tower's archway and crossed the threshold, into a place of ice-cold basalt. I climbed the many steps of smooth stone that took me to the top, where my nakedness was bathed in eerie anti-light. The sentient radiance moved in circular fashion, like some revolving behemoth eye, and the pulsing beam of black light shot out toward the moon. I stepped out onto the circular balcony and was surprised to find no metal lattice to keep me from falling to the rocks below. I gazed outward as the moon began to decay in the outer darkness, and as I beheld that dying globe I felt an uncanny need to touch it. Thus I reached out, stepping into the path of black and violet illumination that beamed toward the decrepit globe. I walked into the aether, toward the dying moon, as cosmic mistral frolicked with my hair and encased my mortal nakedness. The blackness all around me began to ripple like waves of an ocean, and I smiled as this nameless undulation washed me outward, toward an infinity of naught.

XXVIII

He left his apartment at around twenty minutes to midnight on August 29th, with a yellowed newspaper cutting in his hand. It was his hope that most of the Caucasians that inhabited the section of the metropolis where he had found a hotel would be inside at so late an hour; for he had grown to hate the suspicious glances from their pallid faces when they noticed him, and he loathed the way they infested the sidewalks, oozing like puffy pale maggots as they chattered in high nasal tones. Thus he rushed beneath the bright windows of occupied buildings that were hideous in their modernity, and he scowled at the bleating voices and obnoxious contemporary noise that was the music of the age that squeezed from out those windows and maddened him. He had rushed quickly and was soon breathless, and so he finally ceased his scurrying and leaned beneath one antique lamp post that looked different from the ones that illuminated the populated places, and as he calmed his lungs he brought the cutting to the light and examined it anew. It was because of the article he had found in the old newspaper, and more specifically the accompanying photograph, that he had come to the city; for in the photograph he saw a thing that had visited him in his most fantastic dreams, a statue carved of dark wood that resembled a bestial black goddess, a loathsome thing of Africa. In his fantastic dreams he was one among a throng of the very old folk who worshipped this effigy of twilight, and it astounded him to discover, quite by accident in the bookshop where he was employed, a page of newspaper that had lined a box of books that were a part of a dead man's library, the image from his midnight dreams. The books in the box were decades old and of little value, and he had been bored to death as he plucked them from the box and listed them in his notebook; and he had barely noticed the folded sheet of newsprint at the bottom of the box until its photograph seized his attention. He read the article that spoke of the old abandoned section of a city, and of its courtyard where a mysterious pagan statue stood like some thing of secret myth. Thus he had come to the ugly modern city, determined to discover its neglected older corners and the courtyard with the aid of a street map.

As he leaned against the lamp post the midnight air was graced with a soft low sound—a bell was tolling in the centuried church he could dimly see in the distance, and the genteel pealing helped to take him away from the neoteric clamor of the city and its plastic inhabitants. He followed the sound into the shadowed confines of the older section, where he was suddenly overwhelmed with a

Some Unknown Gulf of Night

sense of keen expectancy; for he felt that another world was opening before him, an elder realm of old wood tainted by strange sunsets and ghastly moon-fire, where one could encounter neglected deities, forgotten gods. Paved sidewalks were replaced by cobblestone that led him, at last, to the arched threshold and the sacred place beyond it. Lured, he stepped into an older shadow and breathed another air that was fragrant with spice and marvel, and in that air he thought he could detect half-heard songs that were a paean of rapture that called the thing, darkly divine, whose worship had elapsed, the thing whose idol was suddenly before him. He knelt below the hoary figure of a goddess carved of obsidian and ached to chant the half-heard mantra that haunted his skull. He breathed the alien language and drifted into an incorporeal place disembodied from mundane reality. The hand that stroked his hair was as smooth as polished marble, and as chilly. Taking that hand in his, he kissed it; yet as he stood to drink in her spectral beauty, his eyes were burned by the awful whiteness of the moon above them. He stared at her with prayerful eyes, and so she turned from him and moved a hand into distant air, forming a rift in reality beyond which he could see the others of his ancestral kin, the strange dark folk who hungered to dance around their goddess. Taking his hand, she led him through the threshold of dream, into which, happily, there would be no return.

XIX

    The wretched birds, happy and chattering, fly over the house of dream. It was there that I was content, when once I lived, there where I pressed pen to paper and evoked my dreams with poetry and prose. The shuttered windows of the age-old walls kept out the light of modern day, and when my hands smoothed the fine antique wood with which my furniture was composed I could touch the past. I breathed in uncommon air, shadow-tainted and fragrant with forgotten things that I could touch and taste. When I closed my eyes I could journey where I would, to temple groves where interlaced boughs conjured shadow through which to drift, along cool paths where vague forms watched and waited. Within my mind I could hear the last song of youth, and sense the wind upon the waters beneath which an alien thing, crowned like Medusa, called my name. Winged beings that were not the wretched happy birds would rove through dark air, accompanied by the peals that shuddered forth from elder

Some Unknown Gulf of Night

towers, and together these sounds would coax remembered song from mortal mouth. But phantoms have no mouths with which to sing, and spectres do not sleep or dream. We walk the wind through a realm of nothingness, dismembered shadows without form or feeling, wanting so to taste, just once again, the dreaming that belongs to they still living.

XXX

   I followed the heartbeat of my vision, out of raw reality and into another place beyond the rim of time and space. The plastic city of mortality crumbled behind me, a lifeless memory, and there spread before me mists of light that clothed an elder realm, a town where centuried roofs huddled beneath golden sunset beams. This was a locality where I could catch exhausted exhalation and drink with lungs a senescent elixir of unearthly mist, where the shadows of my eyes, no longer writhing in agony at the sight of neoteric glare, could blend with deeper darkness. I stood upon a hill from which one was rewarded with a panorama of a sunset city where ancient houses crowded centuried lanes, where wraiths of shimmering radiance played among the Georgian steeples of slumbering oratories in which pilgrims uttered prayers. Oh, how I longed to articulate such rare language, to chant to elder gods; but I had no tongue with which to pronounce such benedictions, and my only vocal sounds were hateful hiss and

Some Unknown Gulf of Night

moronic moan. Thus I backed away from the edge of the hill on which I stood and looked, following the path of sod that took me out to the lane that led me to the another kind of sacred house—the residence in which my god of fiction had penned his poetry and prose. It rose before me, the grey Victorian house, which I had seen in waking, but to behold it here, in dream, was an added enchantment; for this was a demesne in which time and space did not exist, and I knew that the house would still be standing here, enshrouded with the orange and amber rays of sunset, when man's little world was naught but a burned-out cinder. For dreams can never die. I saw that the door of the lower room, where he had lived and worked, was open, and I could feel the keen imaginative lure coax me to it; but I did not need to enter its confines in order to drink the rich elixir of imagination and art, because that art was its own entity, existing in the mundane world of mortality as well as in this realm. His weird fiction was devoured by eyes of flesh, was spoken by mouths of human tissue; it tainted the minds of women and men and sank them into a void of such phantasy as they had never known. It brought them here, to the place where I stood, beguiled.

I shut my phantom eyes and remembered his work, as encroaching twilight darkened the abyss above me. I entered a dream within a dream, wherein six strange stars winked awake as they clustered around a sallow moon. As I pierced that gulf of night with my eye-beams, I saw a portion of its gloom drift to the place before me, where there was no longer a house of wood but rather a site of nameless ritual where seven pillars tilted over an altar around which six shadow-figures stood. The essence of my dreaming self sifted through dark aether toward the altar, and soon I was reclined upon its smooth and chilly stone.

One of the figures, hooded and obscure, was taller than the others, and it tilted its lean and blurry form to me as it spoke. "Ah, the seventh dreamer. We have awaited thee from dusk to dusk. We require you to join our chorus and bless the alignment of stars, so that their chaos may envelope the time of mortal men. Speak with us the chant that we now teach you." One by one the other apparitions flowed to me and bent their mouths to mine, and as they whispered into that cavity, my mouth, I felt the fabric of their eldritch language spill beneath my teeth and seek the tongue I did not own. I made my paltry moan in answer to their prayers as sorrow stabbed my soul and slipped as water from my eyes. But then the tall and faceless effigy bent above me, and I saw that it was composed of purest nightmare, black and proud and alien. It was the sublime and dripping eidolon that was one aspect of that genius who was my god of fiction, a phantasm of horror elevated unto the heights of literary art. Ah, how my mouth ached so as to howl orison in honor of this devil now bent over me—but I had no tongue with which to form unholy idiom, and thus I whimpered.

"Your agony is a form of prayer," the old one said with words that issued from him as smoke and ash that drifted to my mouth and coated my face. I watched as the being lifted one dark hand and reached beneath its hood to a place where it should have worn a mouth, and when that hand

Some Unknown Gulf of Night

emerged from the faceless void it held a portion of some black tongue that licked the being's palm. That hand dipped into my mouth and planted the thing of writhing muscle behind my teeth; and I felt the dry rough thing root itself beneath my mouth, a mouth that, now transfigured and bewitched, spoke the prayer of the seventh dreamer, as a strange star formed above us in the haunted place beside the jaundiced moon, a star that began to crawl in assembly with its kindred in honor of our dread lord.

XXXI

Ashton read the letter over a second time and laughed. How delightful to be insulted. Usually the telegrams that he received concerning the publication of his poems, books that were illustrated with photographs of his outré sculptures, had been empty-headed in their prosaic praise; but this new response was a welcome change. "A friend gave me a copy of your *Cthulhu and Others in Stone* as a Yule gift. You are one sick bastard. God knows from what mental cesspool you dredge your polluted ideas." Laughing again, he crumpled the paper and tossed it into the hearth, and as he bent toward the flame the amulet worn around his neck swung against his breast. His hands found the cord and pulled the thing over his head, and he held it to the firelight so that he could admire his work—this icon that he had sculpted from dinosaur bone. Gazing at the amorphous object he whispered to it, "Where do I get my ideas? From Outside, and its secret inhabitants." Delicately, he pressed one hard edge of bone

Some Unknown Gulf of Night

against his forehead and moved it so as to inscribe a kind of sign into his skin, and as he did so he imagined that the firelight dimmed a little, although no current assailed the cabin room. Turning his eyes to one dim corner, he admired his newest work, a figurine fashioned from metamorphic rock. It was larger than his usual study in stone, and in the darkness of its corner its wavering silhouette blended easily with other shadow. The longer he studied it, the more it perplexed him, as had its five kindred—for its amorphous shape would not keep solid form, but seemed to undulate and reform, suggestively. Like its kindred, its design had not been planned; rather, it had taken form beneath his tools and hands, revealing its odd self as he watched with a sense of wonder shining in his captivated eyes. Yes, it had inspired wonder—and subtle fear; for it was a ferocious icon that conveyed a kind of hunger that he could not comprehend. Entranced, he laughed a third time as he drifted to his feet and stalked toward the statuette.

Ashton pressed his hand to the idol's soft stone, and then he took it up with both hands and cuddled it to his chest, where it pressed closer so as to listen to his mortal heartbeat. The poet walked out of the cabin's doorway, into twilight, and found the path that took him into the foothills that were his intimate haunt. He climbed until he reached the stretch of land where a low burial mound rose above the grass, and then he stopped and frowned at the dead tree atop that mound, a dendroid corpse that drooped its withered branches to the ground. It annoyed him to see the black woman who leaned against the tree and chiseled into its dead bark with ritual dagger. She turned to him and motioned that he should join her, and thus he reluctantly crept up the mound until he could smell her fragrance as it washed to him on the wind that moved the soft silk of her yellow dress. She smiled, and he shuddered at how the dead moonlight glimmered on her wet teeth.

She saw the figurine that he held to his chest and cooed. "Ah, the sixth dreamer. Set it in the ring among its fellows while I complete the sign." There was command in her gentle voice, and he yielded to it, falling to his knees next to where the other figurines formed an incomplete circle. What warm emotion he felt as he examined the other creatures of sculpted stone, as if they were familiar cronies who welcomed him as their own. How wonderful to watch their weirdness as it was complimented by the ghastly moon, that awesome disc in the meaningless vortex of night. Ashton heaved his moan into the gathering wind that caught it and took it upward, to the lifeless lunar sphere that grinned down upon the scene. An essence of his moan echoed among the stars.

"Rise," a voice instructed, "and help me nourish this elder creature with mortal wound." Weirdly, he was lifted to his feet, which dragged themselves to the sorceress. He watched her remove her dagger's tip from the tree and studied the emblem that had been engraved upon the bark; and then he watched as the woman showed him her palm, into which she pressed the dagger's blade and etched the arcane symbol into her flesh. The wind blossomed into tempest that caused the woman's long red hair to billow as she floated to him and pressed her wet

Some Unknown Gulf of Night

red hand against his mouth, which drank her acrid blood, the taste of which coiled within his mouth and, rising, taunted his brain with scalding vision. Her mouth, so close to his, breathed alien language into his own, and then her fingers clutched at his hair and smashed his face against the dead tree's husk, which he bathed with blood. Ashton wrapped his arms around the trunk and held steadfastly as the creature beside him tore his shirt from his body and bit into his back. He felt her alchemical hands knead his flesh. "We welcome the seventh dreamer," she informed him as his flesh shifted and reshaped. Firmly, she held his altered form to the moon, and then she planted him in the circle among his kindred, with whom his now liberated limbs moved in danse. And as he capered he could see the shifting of starlight and hear reverberations from beneath the mound. He saw the centuried tree that moved with them, twitching its branches as they grew thick and dark with resuscitation. He beheld the globes of searing unearthly color that flowered on those branches, spheres that resembled seven mocking suns; he watched them hatch and scorch the atmosphere with fire that burned the woman's face away, revealing her nothingness that was a representation of future time. Spitting laughter, she joined the seven dreamers in celebration of the Old Ones who, finding portal, filtered beyond dimensional rim from Outside.

XXXI

The black skyscraper towered above him in all its hideousness, reaching toward the filthy smog as in the streets a myriad of cars filled the air with hateful honking. His need to escape became paramount, and thus he rushed from this modern activity toward the old and neglected portion of town, a place that was shunned by most because of its dilapidation, its stench of decay that came, in part, from the place at the bottom of one steep hill where a charnel canal dragged its water through a realm that was always dark with mist and shadow. He tripped down the hill, past the vacant buildings with shattered windows, over pavement littered with grime and shards of broken glass. Slowing his pace, he listened to the silence of the place, which was another reason why the city's mundane inhabitants did not like it—for they found a kind of safety in their clamor, whereas quiet was a thing they could not comprehend, a thing that drove them to distraction. Even the dark water of the lean canal refused to make a noise, and he gazed into its current as he gradually stepped onto the ancient stone of the bridge that crossed the water. Stopping for one moment to study the sluggish flow of water, he saw a pale thing rise to the surface and bump against one side of the stone wall of the canal; and he thought perhaps the malformed thing might once have been human, although he could not be certain as the current caught it and pulled it from his view.

He continued his walk along the other length of old stone and followed the gaunt road that took him to St. Toad's. The pile of stone, black with age, rose within its shroud of fog, a miasma that smelled far sweeter than the foulness belched within the artificial city. He pressed his hand against the squares of rock with which the edifice had been constructed and knew that this stone had not been some false manufacture of mankind—it was an element of earth, cold and real. In calm reverence, he entered St. Toad's and found the statue that awaited him in a place of soft illumination, the chiseled form that wore a pallid mask. She had been expertly composed, and as he kissed one chilly breast he could almost imagine that a pulse reverberated from some place beneath it. Lowering to humble knees, he studied the symbol that had been etched onto her firm palm, a sign that drank the room's pale light and was reflected on his eyes. Shutting those eyes, he tilted to the palm and licked it. He shuddered as the place grew chilly, yet when he went to embrace himself he could not find his mortal frame. He had escaped his husk of solid flesh. Now he wandered through a dimension of dreaming the likes of which he had never experienced. He drifted into a darksome valley and its depth of haunted woodland, beside a foul lake in which suggestive black shapes splashed awfully. The surrounding trees were spotted with unwholesome fungi and phosphorescent patches of moss. Pausing beside the lake he peered into its squalid depths, through which a viscous beast broke, a nebulous thing that wore his face and whistled like a fiend before submerging once again into the undulating perdition.

He rose and watched the illuminated woodland for any sign of movement, but there was none; and yet a presence from the place beckoned and beguiled him, and so he moved into its lonesome places until coming to one tree from which small orbs dangled from low boughs, cloudy globes of crystal with hints of fire at their centers. He saw that these globes were not perfectly round; rather, they had oblate ends which brought to mind a passage that he had scanned in a yellow parchment manuscript of the *Book of Eibon*, which told of a wizard who had owned such a spherical crystal in which he could behold some secrets beyond the rim of sanity. Reaching up to touch one low crystal, he peered at the pinprick of light at its center and saw it blossom into a dream within a dream. He watched, bewitched, the thing that pushed out of earth before him—the gaunt tower of black stone that was octagonal in shape and some sixteen feet in height. Creeping to it, his attention was caught by the characters etched upon its surface, and he lifted his hands so that they moved over those markings as a blind man's might decipher brail. And as his hands smoothed the stone his palms transformed, splitting open as mouths that mewed the language etched on stone. The sound of those syllables made him giddy, so that he bent

Some Unknown Gulf of Night

backward and fell onto the place where there should have been ground; but all he could feel was a continuation of plummeting as the black obelisk melted into a mound of loathsome sentience, a formless mass of slime and poisonous vapors. To look upon this unfathomable horror was to surrender all sanity and every ounce of remaining humanity. Thus he bubbled as a blind amorphous stream of slime that spilled into the swamp of nothingness, where he splashed among his kindred in a mire of meaningless cosmic mud.

XXIII

It wafted to him from the distant harbor, the low and bestial whistling that overwhelmed with desolation. Exiting the café, he stumbled beneath the old roofs that tilted toward the street, past the shuttered windows of strangely tenanted hovels composed of crumbling brick and rotted wood. He paused for one moment before the cloudy window of an antique shop and pressed his face against the cold unyielding glass; and as he peered into the spectral room of forgotten things he thought he could espy a dim silhouette that motioned to him, invitingly. Gazing through the dusky glass had always bequeathed a sense of dreaming, as if the place before him were a realm of vision that could melt his solid flesh and pull him into another place; and he would have allowed himself such alteration if the harbor whistles had not sounded a second time and lured him from the glass and down the lane, past the decaying spire of an abandoned funerary chapel, along the twisting cobblestone lanes on which crumbling warehouses

Some Unknown Gulf of Night

slept within their shrouds of mist and spray.

He slipped onto a wooden pier and leaned on its railing as he peered at the expanse of feculent water, trying not to gag at the fumes that coiled from the floating debris among the carcasses of fowl and fish. One piece of litter strangely caught the reflection of the yellow moon, and as he studied it he thought it was some portion of a leather sail to which had been fastened a pallid mask. He looked at it as the moonlight dimmed, imagining that the flat fabric floating on still water began to ripple, to rise slowly and whistle to him. It shaped itself into a naked human form that walked on water toward the pier, so malignant that he had to shut his eyes and clamp hands over ears. He could not, however, block the stench that rose from the water and settled just before him. Wet hands pressed against his wide forehead and played within his scant hair as something kissed his rector's collar and moaned his name. Raising his hands to push the thing away, he touched the heavy breasts that swung before him as something chilly found his ear and whistled once again.

He opened his eyes and beheld the naked thing that wore a pallid mask. Beneath that façade of silk a voice, low and mesmerizing, sighed to him to join with her as she danced upon the water. "Come with me," it coaxed, "and I will plunge thee into a depth of dreaming such as you have never known." He saw the long steel needles that kept the mask in place, and as he watched a lithe black hand pinched the needle that had been pushed through the mask's mouth and pulled it free. How wickedly the moonlight shimmered on the needle's point, and how cold that needle was as the figure smoothed it across his lips. He watched the hand that removed the other implements that fastened mask to flesh, and when the last needle was removed he raised his hands so as to catch the mask that fell to them. He did not understand why there was no face before him at the place from which the mask had fallen, why there was nothing but smooth black surface that seemed to drink an essence of glimmering moonlight and thus glisten like a pool of oil.

God, how silky was the mask against his fingers! What wonderful fragrance wafted from it, sweet yet pungent, like shards of odor that pierced into his brain. Perhaps if he pressed the mask to his face it would dispel the wretched harbor stench that made him want to vomit. He pushed the perfumed silk to his face and peeked through eyeholes as the black woman's hands drifted to him and began to push the needles that she held through the silken fabric. He uttered no sound as the final pin found his mouth again and pushed through his numbing lips. His eyes remained open as the figure tilted to him and pressed her facelessness against the mask as the wooden pier melted beneath his feet. He thought he could see vaguely through the shadow that engulfed him, see the water on which he danced with his spectral mistress in his arms, the enchantress who kept her promise and dragged him downward, into a realm of immortal nightmare.

XXXIV

    I examined the dead city as our raft drifted down the gaunt canal, and did not like the way its outline suggested awful things that one may witness in diseased dreaming. One could not believe that such a place was inhabited—and yet there came from someplace deep within a sound of muffled and monotonous drumming, deliberate and persistent. I could just see, beyond the filthy fog that hovered over the decaying towers of the metropolis, the expiring orb of day sinking in the darkening sky. Our raft was sailing slowly, and yet it disturbed me to see Bobby standing boldly near its edge, holding on to nothing but the enormous grimoire that he had found in an antique shop somewhere in the necrotic megalopolis. We had almost reached the city's end when I beheld the stone bridge ahead of us that spanned the gaunt canal. I thought that the dark figure who stood at the center of the bridge was waving at us, but as our craft neared her I saw that she was gesturing to the risen moon; and it disturbed me, as we approached the bridge, to see Bobby raise one hand and imitate the dark woman's motion. I peeked to where her face should have been, but all I could discern was undulating shadow beneath the length of rich red hair, and then she was blocked out by the rotting stone with which the antediluvian bridge had been erected.

The city was behind us, and gradually our craft drifted more slowly still, until it floated to an outcropping of rocks and stopped. I marveled at how my young friend hopped nonchalantly onto those slippery rocks and climbed their little height to solid ground. Cautiously, I rose to a standing position on the gently bobbing raft and gingerly stepped onto one flat rock; and as I balanced myself on the stony surface the raft behind me moved away, reentering the black canal and drifting from us down the oily water.

"I don't care for this weird trek you've proposed, Bobby," I informed him. "You told me that we were going to visit a haunt of spectral dream such as I experienced during last night's slumber. Thus far this is nothing like my delicious nightmare. Why you've brought that cumbersome tome is quite beyond me."

It was then that the little imp turned to me and smiled as he had never smiled before, and he opened the heavy book so that its sheets of parchment were illuminated by beams of moonlight. I could not decipher the words that had been etched thereon in minute script, and to stare at it oppressed me with headache and dizziness. I had of late been plagued with an unaccustomed ocular trouble which prevented me from reading fine print, and as I peered at the page I experienced a renewed tugging of nerves and facial muscles. "Look here, Howard," he squeaked, "this is an elaborate description of the way to our desired destination, a diagram of language. It's easily deciphered. Come on, old man—follow me!"

He scampered ahead of me, almost skipping, and I limped after him along the way that led down a dark, half-wooded heath where boulders wore patches of phosphorescent moss. I followed the young creature who was impelled by some obscure sense of quest, until we came to a dark and seemingly familiar woodland, into which we walked. Time passed and at last we came upon a miasmic swamp which seemed to excite my friend. Pointing to an alien-featured tree across the foetid quagmire he yelled, "There—we need to stand before that tree." He studied the squalid water and then, to my astonishment, walked onto it, laughing at my yelp of caution. When I saw that he did not sink into the depths I approached the dank surface and saw the path of large flat stones on which my friend was walking. "Are you coming, Howard?" he called; and so I timidly stepped onto one flat rock and held out my arms in an attempt to balance myself as I followed Bobby across the water. Yet the rocks, large as they were, were slippery with slime, and just as I had almost reached the other side I lost my foothold and fell into thick water. Bobby, standing on grassy ground, shook his head as if I were some pathetic clown, and then he set down his book and offered me his hands, which I took as he pulled me out of the swamp. How strange that other hands beneath the surface, phantasmal and determined, seemed to try to hold onto my ankles and drag me to the nadir of foul water.

W. H. Pugmire

Bobby helped me to the solid ground, on which I dripped. "You're a damn mess," he sadly informed me, and then he seemed to completely forget my existence as he turned to the unfamiliar tree and touched a hand to one of the black spheres that was attached to a low branch. Why on earth did he begin to hum to that queer object, and why did his humming sound so unnatural? How curiously he bent to that black sphere and touched it with his mouth. I began to step toward him and foolishly trod upon his monstrous book, the binding of which was warm and wet. Bending to pick it up I was appalled to see that the hide that served as binding seemed to be perspiring, which caused a cry of disgust to escape my mouth. My noise caught Bobby's attention, and he filtered to me with drowsy motion and relieved me of my burden.

"We're almost there now," he pronounced as he chewed upon the black flesh of the sphere into which he had eaten. I did not like the alteration of his intonation, how it was laced with a kind of buzzing articulation. Nor did I like the way his mouth had widened when he smiled. "I have devoured knowledge and can show you your habitat of vision. Follow me." Although wearied of this game of "follow the leader," I held my tongue and moved my feet, my legs weighed down by the heavy fabric of my soggy suit. Eventually we emerged from the woods upon a table-land of moss-grown rock lit by faint moonlight, and something about the place did indeed seem strangely familiar. Even more recognizable were the rusty tracks of a street-railway, which we followed until we came upon a yellow, vestibule car, such as I had discovered in my unfathomable

Some Unknown Gulf of Night

dream. It was untenanted, as in my dream, and we cautiously boarded it. Bobby, before me, had opened the tome and was reading from it in his peculiar buzzing drone, and the snatches of formulae that he uttered aloud were so frightful that I begged him to stop. He turned to me and revealed the monstrous malformation of his face, which was now a mere white cone tapering to one blood-red tentacle. My mouth was frozen with terror, and I could not understand why his clothes were as drenched as my own, or why the heavy book was in my grasp. Feeling faint, I staggered forward, toward the archway in which the other figure stumbled until its visage touched my own. Howling bestially, I plunged into and through the yielding door of glass, the shards of which ripped my atrocious visage from me. Blind and idiotic, I stomped on the floor of our temporary globe, the blasphemous book pressed against my breast, as I raised my facelessness to the cold and primal stars.

XXXV

She escaped the hidden, silent place of old woodland and saw the sunset over the city's towers. The crimson face of the setting sun bathed her eyes with beauty, and soft wind wafting over the canal came to her, moved into her long red hair and frolicked with the folds of her yellow gown. From the woods behind her she heard a faint buzzing that reminded her of something bad, and so she fled to the stone bridge and began to cross over the canal, stopping midway so as to watch the raft that floated toward her on the water. Of the two figures on the raft, the teenage boy standing near the craft's edge ignored her as he studied the heavy book he held, but the other fellow was staring at her with such a helpless expression that she raised her hand to wave at him and smile. How strange that her motion seemed to increase his worry, and this so annoyed her that she did not turn to watch the raft emerged from under the other side of the bridge, but continued her way toward the sunset city. She stopped on her way to study the faceless statue that stood a little ways from the bridge, and wondered at the book of stone it held in basalt hands. How curious were the symbols etched onto what passed as the leaves of the statue's book, and how her fingers tingled as she ran them over those etched characters as a blind woman would in reading brail. Finally, she turned from the curious statue and advanced toward the city, running her still-tingling fingers against the softness of her silken gown.

She entered the city and walked its oddly narrow cobblestone streets, until coming to the extraordinary edifice that was a funerary chapel whose façade was decorated with carvings of fantastic beings that could exist in dream alone. When she entered the place she was surprised to encounter the smoke of incense, for the place seemed absolutely deserted. Pushing one door of scrolled wood, she entered the chapel chamber, where she found seven stone coffins instead of pews. Upon each oblong box of stone reclined a sculptured figure so lifelike that one could imagine they were the slumbering dead with hands pressed in prayer to some dread lord. She pressed her own cool hands together and whispered words that she had remembered from some obscure book of myth, and it confused her how her language spilled from her as a mist that floated upward, to the roof of beams from which six skeletons swung from lengths of hempen rope. As she watched the subtle danse, the risen moon appeared behind one arched window, throwing her beams onto the things of bone and casting their silhouettes above the altar place.

Wind hummed through crevices in the rotting

walls, like some low moaning of lost souls. She watched the skeletal shadows on the wall, above the spreading sculpture of a tree; and when she stepped onto the altar place she marveled that the fruit that hung from sculpted boughs was real. She plucked one pomegranate from its branch and bit into its tart white pulp, and then she laughed to see the pale worm whose flesh she had almost nibbled. Carefully, she chomped again into the flesh of fruit, as the lengthy maggot fell onto her palm and moved with shaping until it resembled one of the curious symbols that she had observed on the faux page of a book of stone. Lifting her hand, she smoothed the creature into her hair and felt it fall onto the fabric of her neck, where it stretched itself into a fleshy rope that coiled around her and lifted her into the quivering air, to where the others hung.

XXXVI

    I loved the ancient things, for in them I found a trace of some dim essence beyond time and space, of the past which is more alive to me than this dull neoteric age that fancied itself so clever and original. And so I sought and found the olden city whose legend had been whispered among devotees of dark things. I was not disappointed. It was almost impossible to believe that the place had ever been a modern site, for its desolate towers and cobblestone lanes were the very epitome of dead eras. I was enchanted by one forlorn edifice that, upon entering, I discovered to be a kind of funeral chapel. I passed into its nave where there were no aisles but rather seven coffins of stone. The ceiling was covered with a macabre fresco of seven skeletons engaged in danse around a monstrous white worm. I walked on to the altar, where I found a large book bound in red leather; but when I opened the book I found that the script on its yellowed pages was too faint to be read. Turning the brittle leaves, I found a faded photograph tucked into the book, and I studied the image as well as I could, which seemed to be some kind of faceless icon wrapped in a crimson robe. I shut the book and looked around but could not locate the physical representation of the photographic image. Whistling a remembered hymn, I strode out of the building and continued my investigation of the cobblestone lanes, until I came upon what must once have been an antique shop but was now obviously an abandoned ruin. There was no door, and the large window was fissured with age. Peering through the cracked pane, I was startled to see that the cramped room beyond it was still packed with fabulous items. Dim moonlight above me threw my shadow into a dusky corner of the room—at least I thought it was my shadow, although some trick of illusion made it fluctuate with movement as if it were beckoning me to enter inside its confines.

 I crossed the threshold and breathed in the tenuous aether of the silent room. I looked around at the objects from another time, and seemed transported through dimensions that, unlocking, pulled me into other years. The awful glow of the pale, pitying moon crept through window cracks, and in that strange light I sensed another realm press upon my mind, as if I had entered a phantasy of dream. I walked until I found the nameless eikon carved from crimson wood, and it shocked me to realize that it was a representation of the photographed being I had beheld within the church of death. I could not fathom what it might represent, or why its countenance was veiled. I carried it with me as I continued my exploration of the room, and I laughed with delight when I found a kinetoscope with a winding

Some Unknown Gulf of Night

handle, which I rotated as I pressed my face against the viewing screen. What unearthly light began to bloom within the box, in which I beheld the flickering image of six gnomes who capered within a circle of squat stones. They danced like lunatic freaks and banged the backs of their hands to those of their neighbors, and as their talons struck each other there was a play of sparks which illuminated a figure in the background, a thing out of Poe, tall and lean and wrapped in fabrics red as sunset flame. I watched as the figure raised one beckoning hand as the sparks tapped against the glass through which I peered, the surface of which began to crack as had the window of the dismal shop. I felt those sparks spill into my eyes as my hair stood up on end, and for a moment I was blinded by a blackness that seemed to pull me into it. I shut my burning eyes and pushed away from the machine, but as I steadied myself the air around me altered, and the silence of the place was haunted by the faint beating of insistent drums that was accompanied by another throbbing sound, as if I were surrounded by things that danced. And when I opened my eyes I saw the beasts that moved in slanting moonbeams, the creatures of which I was the seventh. We twirled upon the haunted hill, in ghastly light, as the fixt mass that was our world disintegrated into a cloud of dust upon which the Strange Dark One exhaled until we drifted into some unknown gulf of night.